Ivy shook her head. It was time to focus. 'How does this blogger know the truth about vampires?'

'And why does he or she want to expose them?' Olivia asked.

'I don't know,' Ivy said. 'But I know one thing for sure.' She folded her arms, glaring at the blog on her computer screen as if she could laser it with her eyes. 'It's lucky I came back when I did.'

Sink your fangs into these:

MY SISTER THE VAMPIRE

Switched

Fangtastic!

Revamped!

Vampalicious

Take Two

Love Bites

Lucky Break

Star Style

Twin Spins!

Date with Destiny

Flying Solo

Stake Out!

Double Disaster!

Flipping Out!

Secrets and Spies

Fashion Frightmare!

MY BROTHER THE WEREWOLF

Cry Wolf!

Puppy Love!

Howl-oween!

Tail Spin

Sienna Mercer

MY SISTER THE VAMPIRE

STAKE OUT!

EGMONT

With special thanks to Stephanie Burgis

For Jade. Oldest and best friends forever!

EGMONT
We bring stories to life

My Sister the Vampire: Stake Out first published in Great Britain 2012
by Egmont UK Limited
The Yellow Building, 1 Nicholas Road
London, W11 4AN

ISBN 978 1 4052 5988 0

www.egmont.co.uk

A CIP catalogue record for this title is available from the British Library

Typeset by Avon DataSet Ltd, Bidford on Avon, Warwickshire
Printed and bound in Great Britain by the CPI Group

49534/6

Stay safe online. Any website addresses listed in this book/magazine are
correct at the time of going to print. However, Egmont is not responsible
for content hosted by third parties. Please be aware that online content can
be subject to change and websites can contain content that is unsuitable for
children. We advise that all children are supervised when using the internet.

Chapter One

'Strawberry cupcake with pink glitter frosting?'

Ivy Vega had to resist the urge to curl her lips in disgust as Holly thrust an absurdly colourful cake in her face.

'Er, thanks, but no,' Ivy muttered. *There's only so much pink I can be near without coming out in hives.*

Holly's smile didn't falter. It never did. 'Maybe later!' she chirruped, before moving on round the group with her platter. It looked like a rainbow that had fallen to earth and shattered on to the plate in the form of colourful cakes.

Sunshine streamed on to the bright green grass

of Franklin Grove's park but, for once, vampire Ivy didn't mind it one bit. She was just glad to be back in her home town in time to enjoy the last of the summer before school started again. With her twin sister Olivia, her boyfriend Brendan and all their friends happily picnicking around her, Ivy couldn't have felt further from the dark, ancient Transylvanian halls of the super-snooty Wallachia Academy for Vampires. And she couldn't have been happier about that, especially now that Brendan had recovered from the illness that had brought her racing back to Franklin Grove.

He'd had a seriously bad reaction to the oxymistine in his Taurus Bars – the energy snacks he'd been eating – with dire consequences. It was only because of Ivy's skills with essential herbs – learnt from the Transylvanian gardener, Helga – that she'd been able to save his life.

There was just one thing that could have made

their celebration picnic even better: if Ivy had been allowed to talk about everything she was celebrating! Unfortunately, Olivia's new friend Holly was sharing the picnic and, as a certified 'bunny' who knew nothing of vampires, she couldn't be allowed to know the secret.

It's called the First Law of the Night for a reason, Ivy thought.

'Come on, everyone! Try them!' Holly had arrived back in front of Ivy and pressed a fairy cake into her hands. 'Olivia is such an amazing baker!'

Ivy blinked as she accepted the same pastel cupcake she'd turned down only a moment earlier. 'When you said "Maybe later", I didn't think . . .' She trailed off, feeling a mean sentence forming. Then she frowned. 'Did Olivia *really* make these?' For almost as long as Ivy had known her, Olivia had been a total klutz in the kitchen.

Ivy's twin shook her head, laughing. 'Trust me, I'm not that good,' she said. 'I actually got a lot of help from –'

'Don't be silly,' Holly said. 'These cakes are *all* you!' She turned to the rest of the group, flipping her long blonde hair back and setting one hand on the hip of her jeans. Embroidered flowers swirled down her legs like a walking garden, stitched in such bright colours they made Ivy's eyes hurt. 'Don't listen to her, you guys! You know how she's always so modest.'

Brendan smiled politely, and their vampire friend Sophia was barely bothering to pretend that she was listening. Olivia's bunny friend Camilla gave a distracted 'Hmm'. Her blue eyes were unfocused beneath her artistic beret, and she was clearly too busy mentally storyboarding her next movie to care about the finer points of cupcake baking.

Ivy felt herself frown. *I know my own sister. Olivia*

definitely got some help from someone else. Perhaps their bio-dad's fiancée, Lillian?

It didn't really matter who had helped – that wasn't what made Ivy narrow her eyes as she watched Holly going round the group with the platter like a door-to-door saleswoman. No, the real problem was . . .

Why is Holly talking about Olivia as if she's known her forever? When Ivy had left for Transylvania, Holly hadn't even *lived* in Franklin Grove.

'Hey! Earth to Ivy.' Brendan scooted closer, pulling a Tupperware box out of his backpack. 'Olivia's not the only one who's been baking.'

'Don't tell me you've turned into a master chef too.' Ivy took the box and started to peel back the lid as Holly started an enthusiastic conversation with the rest of the group about pastries. 'I wasn't gone *that* long – *Oh!*' Ivy's mouth dropped open. Inside were the most perfect, smooth orbs of sugary almond goodness. 'Macaroons! For me?'

Brendan grinned, his dark hair flopping over his forehead. 'Don't you think I know what you like?'

Ivy shook her head, amazed. Instead of the usual pinks and greens, these macaroons were blood red. *Gorgeous.* Ivy sighed in wonder – each macaroon was wrapped in its own ribbon, and each ribbon had bats printed on it. *Brendan knows me so well*, she thought. *These are perfect.*

'I just wanted to do something really special to welcome you back from Transylvania,' said Brendan. Then he smiled. 'I kinda missed you, you know.'

'Me too,' Ivy said, her throat suddenly tight.

She'd gone to Wallachia Academy to keep her grandparents happy and have a 'proper' vampire education, but it hadn't taken long for her to realise that it had been a big mistake. Her uber-traditional grandparents might never understand, but Ivy knew that a boarding school thousands of miles from her twin and her boyfriend could never be the right place for her.

She wanted to tell Brendan this, but she knew she was skating on the thin ice of Lake Mushy. Quickly, she unwrapped a macaroon. As Brendan watched, grinning, she took a big bite. Her teeth caught on something cold and sharp.

'Ow!' She spat whatever it was out on to a napkin – then stared. It was a bat-shaped ring. Brendan had hidden it in the macaroon! The writing inscribed across its wings read: *I'm batty for you*.

'Oh, ouch,' Ivy groaned. She couldn't help wincing, even as she saw her boyfriend's grin widen. 'Since when are you so pun-ny?'

He shrugged. 'I guess something came over me while you were gone.'

Ivy rolled her eyes. 'Like a fungus?'

'Or a pun-gus.' Brendan smirked shamelessly.

'Hmm.' She narrowed her eyes at him. 'Tell

me the truth. Were you really sick? Or was it just a bad case of a-*pun*-dicitis?'

Brendan snorted. 'If it was, it must have been contagious.'

Ivy shook her head. 'That's it,' she said, in between giggles. 'I'm stopping now before the contagion spreads any further.'

'Just don't go away again,' Brendan said, placing an arm around her shoulders. 'Then we should all stay safe.'

'Got it.' Ivy slipped the ring on the ring finger of her right hand. A perfect fit.

Brendan bumped shoulders with her. 'I know,' he said, 'you don't like loads of mush and romance.'

'To say the least,' Ivy said firmly. Still, she couldn't help stroking one finger over the little face of the bat on her ring. She looked up into Brendan's eyes and found him grinning at her.

'Don't worry,' he said. 'I thought your return

home was important enough to mark, but from now on –' Brendan crossed his heart – 'I promise, you're going to be totally ignored and overlooked. Just the way you like it.'

'You better,' said Ivy, biting the insides of her cheeks to keep a dumb smile off her face. 'I have something for you too.'

Nearby, Camilla jumped up, breaking into the Great Pastry Debate. 'Come on, guys! Split into two groups, and pretend those sticks over there are swords. I need to figure out the choreography for my fight scene! Ivy, are you two on-board?'

'Not this time.' Ivy waved Camilla off. As the others took up formations under Camilla's direction, laughing and fencing with the sticks they'd picked up from the grass, Ivy and Brendan scooted to a more sheltered spot. As soon as they were safely out of cupcake range – and, she hoped, out of sight as well – Ivy reached into her black rucksack and pulled out the gift she'd felt almost too embarrassed to bring along. She didn't want any observers for this one.

'*The Dead Travel Fast*?' Brendan said. Now he was the one gaping in amazement. 'This is my favourite book!'

'I know that, dummy.' Ivy rolled her eyes as she dropped it in his lap, glad she had her back turned to the others. 'Do you think I would have got it otherwise? It's a first edition copy.'

'A first edition, huh?' Brendan raised his eyebrows in mock outrage. 'Ivy Vega, you are a total fraud. You may pretend to be tough, but inside you are as soft as Holly's cupcakes.'

'Whatever!' Ivy groaned. But she didn't resist when he pulled her into a quick hug.

Wow. Olivia hid a grin as she quickly looked away from Ivy and Brendan. *I've never seen Ivy so loved-up!* Usually her sister put on such a front of carelessness; sometimes it could be hard even for

Olivia to guess at her feelings. Right now, though, Ivy and Brendan were smiling into each other's faces with pure delight.

It must be true love, Olivia thought. *Of course, true love is easy. Not like me and Jackson, with all the distance and* . . .

'Excellent!' Camilla said, and waved for everyone to set down their 'swords'. 'That'll definitely work on-screen.'

Olivia hid a smile. That was Camilla – she might have spent the last half hour in a world of her own, caught up by the new movie idea in her head, but now that she was wide awake, she was back in full director-mode. Olivia didn't mind being bossed about a bit to make her friend happy, though. Camilla had been partly responsible for Olivia meeting her ex-boyfriend, Jackson, when they'd got jobs on a film set in Franklin Grove.

Jackson . . . *Don't think about him!*

'Let's play Frisbee!' Olivia called, looking for any distraction she could find.

As the group arranged themselves to play the new game, she caught Ivy's eye and the two of them smiled. *Ivy's back where she belongs*, Olivia thought. *Camilla's in boss-mode. Brendan's healthy. Everything's back to normal.*

Almost . . .

'Catch!' Brendan called, as he threw the Frisbee. It arced over Holly's head. The new girl jumped into the air, but she missed it by at least three metres. The Frisbee landed just short of the park gates, and Holly's shoulders slumped.

Olivia shook her head. *That's a really short throw, for Brendan!* Normally, Brendan would have been able to throw that Frisbee *way* out of the park with his vampire super-strength. Not that any of them could let on about this in front of Holly – vampire secrets needed to stay just that. Olivia was lucky to be in on the secret, but she had to

12

keep it, just like the vampires did.

Some of the group couldn't resist a bit of teasing, though. 'Not back up to your usual strength yet, Brendan?' Ivy teased.

'Maybe you need a bit more rest, huh?' their friend Sophia added, laughing as Brendan flushed.

Holly's voice cut through all the teasing: 'What are you guys talking about?'

Uh-oh, Olivia thought. She turned and saw her new friend staring at the rest of them as if they were speaking gibberish.

'That went really fast and really far,' Holly said, looking over her shoulder. 'How could he ever throw further than *that*?'

'Oh, that was just . . .' Olivia said, her words falling away into a long, drawn-out 'uuhhhh' sound, '. . . an inside joke!'

Holly smiled uncertainly back at her. 'Oh, OK. Um, yeah, funny . . . I'll just go get the Frisbee.'

Guilt tightened Olivia's chest as Holly walked

away, the embroidered flowers on her jeans glinting in the sunlight. Olivia knew all too well what it was like to feel an outsider in Franklin Grove. The last thing she wanted was to make her new friend feel that way.

As she turned back to the others, she saw the vampires in their group – Ivy, Brendan and Sophia – exchanging warning glances. The First Law of the Night said their existence must never be revealed to outsiders. Holly wasn't like Camilla, who'd lived around vampires for years and no longer noticed or questioned the fact that her classmates could run super-fast. Holly was new to Franklin Grove. She was a true outsider.

And she was smart.

As Holly picked up the Frisbee, Ivy walked quickly over to Olivia. Something sparkled on her hand, catching Olivia's attention.

'Oh, wow. Ivy, did Brendan just give you a –'

'Why did you invite her along?' Ivy interrupted.

14

'I thought we were supposed to be relaxing with the gang today. Now I have to be super-cautious so that *Holly* doesn't guess anything. One little bit of teasing and she's already starting in with the awkward questions.'

Olivia suddenly didn't feel like complimenting her sister on her gift any more. 'You know, Ivy, you didn't have to tease Brendan in front of her . . .'

'I just wanted to have a bit of fun with my boyfriend!' Ivy protested. 'Is that off-limits now, with her around?'

'Oh, come on!' Olivia crossed her arms over her pale pink minidress, her guilt turning into irritation. 'I'm not going to just dump Holly now that you're back. She was really supportive when you were away. You should try to be nice to her.'

'I don't mind being nice,' Ivy said. 'But I've only just come home. Can't I take one day to relax and be myself?'

'You *are* in the middle of a public park,' Olivia said, as a jogger ran past them, and a pair of dogs barked madly from the other end of the field. 'You guys couldn't show off your super-skills that much here anyway.'

'But – oh, never mind. Here she comes.' Ivy went back to her place in the park, her scowl just as black as her *Shadowtown* T-shirt and combat trousers.

Brendan threw Olivia a questioning glance. She shook her head as if to say all was good, which it was – the twins never truly fell out. Olivia wasn't sure they were capable!

The group carried on playing, but the atmosphere had definitely changed. When Holly threw the Frisbee to Sophia, Sophia made a hopelessly pathetic attempt to run for it and then gave up, mournfully shaking her head. Even a human could have run faster than that. Olivia saw Ivy grimace at Sophia's play, but even Ivy knew the rules. When Brendan threw her the Frisbee overhand, she barely even tried to reach for it. And when Camilla yelled that she had to be getting home soon, all the vampires in the group slumped with obvious relief.

'Oh, do we have to stop?' Holly said. She was panting with effort, the sleeves of her peasant-style blouse rolled up above her elbows, but she waved the Frisbee enticingly. 'Come on, we were just getting warmed up!'

'Sorry,' said Sophia, collapsing gracefully to the ground. 'I'm, erm . . . winded.'

'Yeah.' Ivy dropped to the ground, groaning. 'I couldn't take any more exercise.'

'Well, OK then.' Holly sighed and set down the Frisbee.

Thank goodness, Olivia thought, as they all sank back down on to the picnic blanket and the grass around it. *Now we can be normal again. And maybe*, she thought, as she saw Holly give Ivy a hopeful smile, *Ivy and Holly can finally have a real conversation.*

Olivia knew Ivy would like Holly if she only gave her a chance. After all, the first time Olivia and Holly had met, Holly had reminded her of her sister! They were both so strong and smart, and both completely determined to launch their writing careers. While Ivy wanted to be an investigative journalist, Holly wanted to become a travel journalist. In fact, Holly had been really keen to interview Ivy about her time in Transylvania. It was almost as though Holly had Ivy on a pedestal!

And now all Ivy can do is ignore her, Olivia thought. Wrapped up in Brendan, Ivy hadn't even noticed Holly's smile, much less returned it.

Maybe once a real conversation started, though, they would finally connect.

'That was just like a scene in that hot new vampire book, *Bare Throats at Sunset,* wasn't it?' Holly said, as she knelt back down on the picnic blanket. 'You know, when all the friends play a game of touch football, just before one of them –' she lowered her voice dramatically – 'succumbs to the vampire's bite!'

'Oh my gosh, you're totally right!' Camilla exclaimed. She had been lying down, but now she popped up again, her blonde curls springing in all directions. 'Do you remember that book, Ivy? It's the one I found through that cult reading group I joined – it picks out books no one else has ever heard of. It would make a fantastic movie!'

'No way,' Ivy groaned. 'I hated that book! Seriously, there's a *reason* that one hasn't hit the bestseller charts. No way would I pay good money for a cinema ticket for any film based on it. I have some taste.'

Olivia winced as she saw Holly's smile drop into a slight scowl. Holly pointed at the *Shadowtown* T-shirt Ivy was wearing. 'Oh yeah? Would you call *that* show high-quality storytelling?'

Uh-oh, Olivia thought. Everybody knew

that *Shadowtown* was hilariously terrible, with its hundreds of amnesia storylines and secret vampire babies. But Ivy was an utterly devoted fan anyway.

Olivia watched the struggle on her twin's face. 'Well, it's . . . I mean, I just . . . I don't like following the crowd. Is that OK?'

'Sure,' Holly said, smoothly. 'I'm just curious about what other people like reading. We obviously have very . . . *different* tastes.' She tried to smile, but Olivia could see it was an effort.

Poor Holly, she thought. *All she was doing was trying to have a conversation about films and books!*

'Yeah, pretty different,' Ivy agreed. 'Personally, I think *Bare Throats at Sunset* is so bad, the author should be arrested!' She crossed her arms, as though challenging anyone to disagree with her.

Holly shrugged, turning the Frisbee over and over in her hands. 'I don't think many people would share your opinion,' she said quietly. Olivia had to give her marks for standing up for herself.

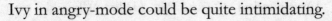

Ivy in angry-mode could be quite intimidating.

'Oh, yeah? Well, let's poll the group.' Ivy swung around to face the others sitting on the blanket. Most of their friends were either looking at the ground or turned away. 'Come on: book debate!'

It was the first time in Olivia's life that she'd ever actually hoped for a sudden, freak thunderstorm – regardless of what it would do to her hair, or how badly it would ruin her dress. She tipped her head back to look desperately at the sky. *Anything* to interrupt this conversation!

What had got into Ivy? Not only was she already fighting with Olivia's new friend, but they were fighting about *vampires*. Who knew how close to the truth they might wander?

'Ah, I thought the book was . . . OK, I guess,' said Sophia. Her fashionable sunglasses shielded her expression.

Brendan shrugged, sliding a nervous glance at Ivy. 'It was . . . quite enjoyable. I suppose.'

Ivy growled. 'Come on, Holly. What do you have to say?'

Holly had kept her head bowed, polishing the Frisbee with her T-shirt as the others talked. Now that she finally looked up, though, Olivia could see that her cheeks were flushed.

'Sorry,' she said. 'I've got to go. There's something I forgot to do at home.'

Olivia started to get up. 'Are you sure? If you want any help –'

Holly said nothing. She just walked away quickly, waving a hand in farewell.

Olivia watched her leave, feeling her shoulders sag. *This isn't how the day was meant to be.* She had to find a way to make Holly feel more a part of the group. But what could she do? She looked down at the picnic blanket, and the cakes that Holly had carefully arranged on a plate.

Well, she thought, *Holly did seem really keen on my baking . . .*

'Hey, everyone.' Olivia turned back and gave the rest of the group her best Hollywood smile, trying to block out the scowl on Ivy's face as she watched Holly leave. *Tomorrow*, she thought. *I'll fix everything tomorrow.* Olivia just had to set her plan in motion.

'How about a baking party?' she said.

She was pleased to see Ivy's eyes light up immediately.

'Great idea! I'll make some of these macaroons – they're yummy. So moreish.' Ivy was looking pointedly at the macaroons and then at Brendan, back at the macaroons and straight into Brendan's face again.

She may as well be waving a placard in the air saying, 'Please start eating normally again, Brendan!' Olivia thought.

He smiled and shook his head. 'I don't know, Ivy,' he drawled. 'They're kinda difficult to bake, you know. Takes someone who really

23

knows what they're doing.'

Olivia held her breath and waited. She watched her sister's cheeks as they went from pale to pink to red, her hands clenching and unclenching.

'I'm sure I can try,' Ivy said after a long pause, her voice all sweet and un-Ivy. Olivia was shocked. *Ivy must really want to be nice to Brendan now that she's back.*

His shoulders were shaking with suppressed laughter, then he burst out into a fit of coughing and had to turn away. When he straightened back up, he looked from one twin to the other.

'Sounds like a great idea!' he announced. 'When do we start?'

Chapter Two

An hour later, the twins were sitting in front of the computer in Ivy's bedroom, surrounded by posters of Ivy's favourite metal band, The Pall Bearers, and beautiful art prints of Transylvanian castles and clouds of bats.

Even the comfort of her favourite decorations didn't make Ivy feel any happier about the task Olivia had set her: emailing Holly to invite her to the baking party. On the way home from the park, Olivia had persuaded Ivy that the invite should go from the two of them together.

'It'll smooth things over,' she'd said. 'You'd really like her if you gave her a chance. Who knows – you might even bond over cupcakes. Maybe you'll teach her to like red and black icing!' Eventually Ivy had agreed.

Of course I did, Ivy thought, and shook her head ruefully. *When have I ever managed to resist Olivia?* From the outside, Olivia might look like the softer, gentler twin, but she had a core of solid steel, especially when it came to making others happy.

'I hope it goes well,' Olivia said now, nervously biting her lower lip. Sunlight streamed into the room past the dark-red curtains, making her pink minidress and strappy sandals look even more out of place against the black-painted walls and goth decor of Ivy's room.

'As long as Brendan *eats*, I'll be happy,' Ivy said. *That* was the important thing about this baking party, she reminded herself, even if it did mean having to hang out with Holly again: it would be the perfect opportunity to feed Brendan up after his illness. He hadn't eaten a thing at the park – not even his own macaroons! She sighed as she watched Olivia type the email message from both of them. 'Did you notice how he –'

Her words were cut off by the sound of Olivia's phone buzzing to life. Ivy couldn't help seeing the name on the display as the phone vibrated beside the keyboard. Her gaze flew to her sister's shocked expression.

Jackson's calling!

'I'll just . . .' Olivia picked up the phone, staring at it as if it were a wild animal that might attack her at any moment. The pop-song ringtone sounded a second time. 'I'll just . . .' she said again, before hurrying out of the room and closing the door.

A moment later, Ivy heard her sister murmuring in the hallway. *He'd better not hurt her again*, Ivy thought fiercely. She liked Jackson, but it had taken Olivia ages to recover after his megastar lifestyle had driven them apart. Seeing her sister upset was pretty much the one thing Ivy could not bear.

Biting down on her worry, she distracted herself with Holly's email:

Come if you want, but don't feel you HAVE to . . .

Sigh. Of course she couldn't really say that, no matter how much she wanted to. Instead, she deleted and started again, summoning some of Olivia's cheerleader pep:

We'd love to see you!!!

Were three exclamation points too obviously fake? Ivy tapped one black-nailed finger on her desktop, trying to make up her mind.

Before she could make any changes, though, Olivia stepped back in the room, looking as if she'd seen a ghost.

'That was Jackson,' she said. 'Did you know it was Jackson? You probably knew it was Jackson.'

'Well –' Ivy began.

Olivia didn't wait to let her answer. 'He was calling from a photo shoot, and he said it made him think of me.' She perched on the edge of the chair beside Ivy, almost shivering with tension. 'Do you think that means something? It probably doesn't mean anything. But . . .'

Her words were tumbling over each other so quickly, Ivy gave up on trying to break in. Olivia might not have vampire super-strength, but right now she was talking with full vampire-style super-speed.

'He said the shoot was themed around dreams coming true, and it made him wonder . . . didn't my dreams come true when I went to Hollywood?'

Ivy winced, thinking of Olivia's starring role in the movie *Eternal Sunset*. The only thing 'eternal' about the movie was the delays caused by Hollywood industry strikes. The movie had been put on hold indefinitely and Olivia's dreams of building a career had stalled. She'd come back home and Jackson had moved on with his celebrity life. Now Olivia was stuck in limbo – or Franklin Grove, as they usually called it.

'He sounded really wistful, like . . . like he was missing me.' Olivia's eyes glimmered, but she didn't cry. Instead, she talked even faster. 'I didn't know what to say to that. So I thought, just to break the tension, I'd mention that book Holly was talking about at the picnic.'

'*Bare Throats at Sunset*?' Ivy groaned. 'Now there's a romantic subject.'

'That's not the problem.' Olivia shook her head. 'He said he'd look out for it, but Ivy – the strangest thing of all was what he said just before hanging up.' She finally stopped talking, her blue eyes wide and filled with panic.

Ivy frowned, feeling all her protective instincts rising. *Hollywood mega-star or not, if Jackson Caulfield has said or done anything to hurt my sister . . .*

'He warned me to look out for vampires.'

'What?!' Ivy's jaw dropped open.

'I know!' Olivia nodded. 'I was so shocked, but I still managed to bluff. I said, "What vampires?" But then he asked me, hadn't I seen his chirps?'

Ivy was already twisting around to her computer to load Jackson's BirdChirp account. BirdChirp was an online social networking group that almost everyone had an account with, from A-list stars to people as normal as the twins. *Well, if you can call us normal,* Ivy thought, remembering all the scrapes they managed to get into.

'What were his chirps?'

'He said there's this funny blog that's become a bit of a viral hit . . .' Olivia's voice trailed off as Ivy clicked Jackson's latest link and a new web page flashed up. Its header made Ivy immediately feel her skin prickle with sweat.

Vampires . . . in Franklin Grove!

'Oh no,' Olivia whispered. She slumped on to Ivy's coffin-bed.

Ivy couldn't speak. She scrolled down the web page, horror sending chills across her skin as she read.

'If you think vampires only live in horror stories or Transylvania, think again. They're here, they're in the heart of America, and they're walking the streets of Franklin Grove. Don't believe us? Then get your teeth stuck into our weekly update on vampire sightings that will make your BLOOD run cold . . .'

Ivy stared at the screen, reading the same words over and over again. 'Jackson's been chirping about this?'

'And millions of people follow him,' Olivia said softly.

'No wonder the blog's gone viral.' Ivy felt sick as she looked down at the hundreds of comments listed under the most recent entry. 'At this point, it's practically an Internet disease.'

Especially where vampires are concerned.

'What are we going to do?' Olivia said.

Ivy stiffened her shoulders. 'We'll take our own Internet action,' she said. 'We have to get on the Vorld Vide Veb and send a batsqueak.' It was the VVV equivalent of a BirdChirp, and Ivy couldn't think of any faster way to spread the message among vampires. 'We have to alert our whole community about the danger.'

Olivia nodded, looking determined. 'They'll have to keep an eye out for this blogger, whoever it is.'

'And be careful not to do anything too vamptastic.' Ivy grimaced. 'No more super-powered games of Frisbee, I guess.'

'Not unless you can all control your strength.' Olivia got up from the bed and stood beside Ivy. 'But it's going to be OK. Now that we know what's going on, you guys can protect yourselves.'

'That still doesn't answer the *real* question . . .'

said Ivy, staring at the signature at the end of the blogger's post.

'*Your brave reporter in the heart of Franklin Grove.*'

Ivy shook her head. *That could be anybody – literally*. It was time to focus. 'How does this blogger know the truth about vampires?'

'And why does he or she want to expose them?' Olivia asked.

'I don't know,' Ivy said. 'But I know one thing for sure.' She folded her arms, glaring at the blog on her computer screen as if she could laser it with her eyes. 'It's lucky I came back when I did.'

No matter how hard she tried, Olivia couldn't make her nerves stop being so . . . nervy. The wistfulness in Jackson's tone as he'd talked about their perfect time in Hollywood, back when she'd really believed that they would be together forever . . . What with that *and* the vampire blog to deal with, she felt as jumpy as a real bunny.

There was only one thing for it: baking!

'Come on!' she said. She led Ivy downstairs into the kitchen and pulled out two aprons from a drawer. 'I want to test out a few recipes. Nothing major. I just don't want to mess up at the party tomorrow. Here –' She pushed one of the aprons into Ivy's hands. 'This one's for you.'

'Wow . . .' Ivy looked down at the apron she'd been given, made of black denim with studs running along the hem. 'It's perfect!' Then she looked up and frowned at the apron Olivia was fastening around herself, which had a pink gingham ruffle around the hem and a sweetheart-shaped pocket. 'Actually, so is yours.'

'It really is, isn't it?' Olivia tied the straps with a bow. *Neat and tidy and perfect. If only my life could be the same!* She brushed her hands together. 'Now –'

'Just a minute,' Ivy said. 'First, tell me how come we have two perfectly suited aprons just lying about in my kitchen, when we've never done any baking here before? How do I know you're really my sister, and not some body-snatched doppelganger?'

Olivia felt her skin heat up in a blush as she gave a nervous giggle. She knelt down quickly to hide her face as she rummaged through the pots and pans. 'Lillian's mom came to stay for a weekend and brought her sewing machine. That's where the aprons came from. No big deal. I mean, she *is* going to be our step-grandmother.'

'Aha . . .' Olivia could tell Ivy hadn't missed the blush. 'Talking of Lillian, it's time for you to come clean about those cakes you made.'

Oops! 'I don't know what you're talking about,' Olivia said. But she already had a guilty grin tugging at her lips.

'Come on,' Ivy said. 'I don't care what Holly claimed – you did not make those cupcakes on your own. I've seen you in the kitchen – you look more lost than me in an organic food store!'

Olivia grinned. 'OK, I confess,' she said, and stood up, holding a stack of measuring cups in her hands. 'Lillian *may* have spent some time in the kitchen with me and Holly. But that's why Holly was being so nice about my baking – she knows how bad I was to start with.' Seeing Ivy's face twitch, she rolled her eyes. 'Oh, come on, Ivy! Give the girl a break. She was just trying to be kind.'

'Whatever.' Ivy gave an unconvincing smile. 'You know, I'm still feeling pretty tired and frazzled after everything that happened at the Academy. I guess it must be making me grumpier than usual.'

Olivia opened her mouth to joke: *Do you really think that's possible?* But on seeing Ivy's face, she stopped herself.

If anyone had the right to be cranky at the moment, it was Ivy.

By the time their bio-dad came home an hour later, both girls were covered in flour and licking out the bowls as they waited for their cakes to finish baking. When he stepped into the kitchen, Olivia winced, expecting him to sigh and complain about the mess. Charles Vega was nothing if not immaculate at all times.

'Don't worry . . .' she began.

But he was too busy muttering to himself to hear her. 'Butter icing or cream-cheese icing? *Butter icing or cream-cheese icing?*'

'Um . . .' Olivia turned to Ivy, her eyebrows raised. Ivy had grown up with Charles. Maybe she understood the question.

Ivy only shrugged. 'Dad? We were just making –'

'Fantastic!' Charles's eyes lit up as he spotted the cupcakes in the oven. 'You girls are thinking about the wedding catering already!'

This time it was Ivy's turn to say, 'Um . . .?'

38

Sienna Mercer

'Why, you're almost as organised as I am.' He beamed proudly at them both, not even seeming aware of the mess.

'Dad, we need to talk to you,' Ivy said, and from the look in her eye Olivia knew she was going to tell him about the blogger. 'We have a big problem.'

'Not any more.' Charles shook his head wonderingly as he gazed at the baking cupcakes. 'This is perfect. We can do tiers of fairy cakes instead of one huge cake. You girls are so forward-thinking!' He dug a small notebook and tiny gold pen out of his jacket pocket and began scribbling. 'Lillian will love it.'

'Actually, Dad,' Olivia said, 'it's really important that we –'

'But what about the flower arrangements!' said Charles. 'How will they be affected by the fairy cakes?'

Shaking his head and mumbling to himself, he

39

wandered out of the kitchen, leaving Olivia and Ivy to exchange a hopeless glance.

'It's nice that he's so happy,' Olivia said dubiously.

'I guess,' Ivy said. 'I mean, I didn't expect my dad to morph into Groomzilla!'

Both girls laughed, but Olivia caught a glimpse of sadness on Ivy's face. 'What's wrong?'

Ivy grimaced. 'I never thought I'd say this, but . . . I kind of miss "Old Dad".'

Olivia thought of the slightly strict, wise man she'd met a year ago. 'He was certainly different.'

'He's happier now,' Ivy said. 'And I'm happy for him, but . . . "Old Dad" would have listened to us about the blogger. He might even have given us some advice.'

Olivia sighed, understanding exactly what Ivy meant. They would have to deal with this problem on their own.

She jumped as the front door opened again.

'There you both are!' Lillian breezed in, stylish as always in a simple but elegant black dress. 'I was just parking the car up in the garage, but I hoped I wouldn't be too late to see both of you. Something smells good!'

'We're making cupcakes,' Olivia said. 'Just the way you showed me.'

'And let's hope you like them,' Ivy added, 'because Dad's thinking cupcakes for the wedding.'

'Oh, well . . .' Lillian waved one graceful hand in the air and smiled as she pulled a book out of her sleek black bag. 'Whatever everyone else wants. I don't mind.'

As Lillian opened her book, the twins shared a meaningful glance. Olivia could see her own reaction mirrored in Ivy's face. Were brides really meant to be *this* relaxed? She decided to test the waters with another question.

'Have you organised your wedding dress yet?'

'Mmm? What was that?' Lillian looked up from her book, smiling ruefully. 'Sorry, I know it's terribly rude to read while we talk, but I just can't help myself. This novel is amazing! Have you girls read it yet?'

As she held it out to show them, Olivia heard Ivy groan. *Bare Throats at Sunset.* Why was everyone suddenly reading that book? Luckily, Lillian was too busy gushing to have noticed Ivy's reaction.

'I've been telling all my friends back in California about it. You have to try it! But, um . . . sorry, what was it you asked?'

'The wedding dress,' Olivia prompted.

'Oh, I'll check out the sales in a couple of weeks' time,' said Lillian. 'Who knows, I might find something.'

Her gaze slid back down to her paperback. Ivy pointed up towards her bedroom with her baking spoon and shot Olivia a questioning look. Olivia knew what she was asking. Lillian was certainly older and more experienced than they were – it would make sense to ask her for help in dealing with the blogger. But then again, did they really want to disrupt their future stepmom's serenity right now?

Making a decision, Olivia shook her head firmly at Ivy. They already had Groomzilla on their hands – the last thing they needed was for the bride to stress out too.

'Lillian? Is that you?' Charles opened the back door and poked his head inside. 'I need your opinion on something.'

Still holding *Bare Throats at Sunset* in her hands, Lillian wandered idly out into the garden to join him. Charles's voice floated through the open door. 'If we used Option Three for a marquee and Option Four for the seating arrangements –' The door closed behind Lillian, shutting off the sound of his voice.

Watching through the window, Olivia saw that, even though Lillian cocked her head attentively as Charles continued to babble, she continued sneak-reading her book.

Then Ivy poked Olivia's shoulder, distracting her from the show outside. 'Why did you make me stop?' she hissed. 'Lillian would have listened to us. She's not wedding-crazy like Dad.'

'Not yet,' Olivia said. 'But weddings are so stressful, Lillian's crazy moments have to be on the way soon – it's kinder not to bother her with anything just yet.'

'Well . . . actually, you might have a point.' Ivy sighed and joined Olivia at the window.

'I wish I could hear what they're saying,' Olivia said.

'No,' Ivy said. 'You really don't. Trust me.' She tapped her ears, reminding Olivia that she could hear every word with her vampire super-senses.

'It's way too boring and grown-up to be worth eavesdropping on.'

'Still.' Olivia leaned companionably against her sister. 'If I ever get married, I hope I'll be as relaxed as Lillian and as organised as our bio-dad – the best of both worlds.' She sighed wistfully, imagining a wedding dress with a huge, sparkly white train. She would feel like an absolute princess as she walked down the aisle to meet her prince – who would *not*, she told herself firmly, look anything like Jackson, no matter what images her mind conjured up. 'What about you, Ivy? What kind of arrangements do you want when you get married?'

There was a moment of dead silence. Then Olivia turned to see her twin's horrified expression, and they both burst out laughing at the same time.

'Sorry,' Olivia said, almost choking on her

laughter. 'That was a silly question, wasn't it?' The idea of grumpy goth Ivy in a big, billowing white dress . . .

'It certainly was,' Ivy said, wrapping one arm around Olivia's shoulders. 'Ivy plus meringue dresses equals the biggest, baddest mood. On the other hand . . .' She licked her wooden baking spoon with an exaggerated flourish. 'Ivy plus meringues? *Now* you're talking!'

With perfect timing, the oven bell dinged. 'They're ready!' Olivia said, and raced to the oven, pulling on pink oven mitts. Why should Olivia care about unavailable dream-boys or vampire-obsessed bloggers when she had a twin like Ivy at her side?

Plus now there were cakes to eat!

Chapter Three

I vy only wished that she could dismiss the mysterious blogger so easily. A day after they'd first discovered the web site, Olivia was running around like a rabbit who'd been fed energy drinks, getting everything ready for the baking party. Ivy took advantage of her twin's distraction to go up to her room and get back online.

A few moments later, she was grinding her teeth as she finished reading the blogger's latest entry:

'. . . *Is it really true that vampires can't stand garlic? This brave journalist is determined to find out, no matter what it takes — so watch this space!*'

Some poor vampire was going to be in real trouble if they didn't stay on their toes. Ivy still remembered a time she'd mistakenly eaten a pastrami sandwich with garlic in it – she'd taken two days to recover!

How was this blogger actually getting things right? And even more importantly, who *were* they? No matter how much Ivy poked about on the web site, she just couldn't find a clue to his or her identity. Even when she ran the blog through the Vorld Vide Veb, nothing came up except a load of hysterical messages from vampires worried about their secrets being exposed.

Ivy hated to admit it, but they had good reason to worry . . . and she'd just had a nasty suspicion of her own. What if the mystery blogger was actually the journalist Serena Star, back on the vampire case? Calling herself 'The Star of Truth', she'd come dangerously close to exposing the secrets of Franklin Grove before the twins had outwitted her. If she was back for a second shot, that could really spell disaster.

Ivy had to talk to Olivia. Carrying her laptop with her, she headed down to the kitchen – just as the doorbell sounded.

Drat!

Letting out a squeal of excitement, Olivia flew down the hallway to answer it. Sighing, Ivy looked for a safe place to set down her laptop. After all the energy Olivia had put into preparing this baking party, Ivy couldn't ruin it for her. *I'll just have to do my best to put the blogger out of my mind . . . for an afternoon.*

'We're the first ones here!' Sophia said, as she swept into the kitchen in front of a lagging Brendan. Behind him, Camilla was rummaging in her bag. Ivy could guess what she was rummaging for.

'And we've brought ingredients!' Wearing uber-glamorous sunglasses, Sophia waved a shoulder bag that could have come straight from the Prada line-up.

Ivy choked. 'You put flour and sugar in *that*?'

'No, silly. I've brought decorations, to make everything look fabulous!'

As Sophia took out a pile of Tupperware boxes from her bag, full of tiny, crystallised cake decorations shaped like black bats and red castles, Ivy looped one arm around her boyfriend's waist.

'Hope you're hungry!' she said perkily, channelling Olivia's most cheerleader-bright tone.

Brendan gave a half-hearted smile. 'I'm here, aren't I?'

The next moment, Camilla was barking orders from the doorway, her face hidden by her video camera. 'Focus, everyone! This is for posterity.'

They all groaned, but not too hard – they knew Camilla too well to argue. And as Ivy looked around the kitchen, she had to admit it really was a scene worth filming. Olivia had covered every available surface in wipe-clean tablecloths and put out bowls of strawberry and lemon sweets, milk chocolate discs, and pink-and-blue decorations. It was like a picture from a magazine, pretty, neat and perfectly organised – just like Olivia herself.

'Come on, everyone!' Olivia said. 'I've got ingredients for crispie cakes and chocolate-chip cookies.' She pointed at the different stations she'd set up around the room. 'Everyone take their places!'

'Brendan's brought something too,' Ivy said, and nudged her boyfriend even as Sophia got to work on freezer cakes.

Brendan's grin was real this time, as he held out his bag. 'Double-00 flour: the best of the best!'

'Aha.' Ivy's eyes narrowed. 'So *this* was your secret to those unbeatable macaroons, huh?'

I can bake macaroons just as good as his, no matter what he says! Ivy reached for the bag, fired up by her competitive instinct – she hadn't forgotten his challenge! – but Olivia's hand closed around it at exactly the same time. *Oops!* Ivy let go, stepping back to let Olivia take the bag . . . just as Olivia let go, stepping back to let *Ivy* take it.

The two girls' eyes met. Then the bag landed on the kitchen floor, exploding and spraying clouds of flour all over both of them.

Ivy heard Olivia draw in a breath. Sophia gasped – perhaps a little too melodramatically. The flour had fallen fast, but not so fast that one of the three vampires in the room couldn't have caught it before it hit the floor. But with Camilla filming, they had to let the mess be made.

'This is priceless!' Camilla yelled. 'Movie magic!'

'Magic, huh?' As the cloud settled, Ivy looked at her flour-covered twin and began to laugh. *So much for staying neat!* 'You look like the Abominable Snowman.'

'So do you,' said Olivia. 'You're not a goth any more! I can't see a single speck of black on you.'

'Actually,' Sophia said, 'covered in this much flour, even *I* couldn't tell you two apart.'

'And I have it all captured on film,' Camilla said with satisfaction.

The doorbell rang. One of Olivia's white-dusted hands flew to her floury face.

'Don't worry,' Ivy said. 'I'll get it.' Still grinning, she went to the front door. When she glanced back over her shoulder, she could see a trail of white footprints on the carpet.

Maybe it's a good thing Dad is in Groomzilla mode. With any luck, he won't even notice the mess!

She opened the front door and found Holly wearing a sunny yellow top and a wildly colourful skirt. Her long, shining blonde hair was set off perfectly by subtle red streaks, and she was carrying . . . a pizza box?

'Hi!' Holly said. 'Sorry, I don't really have time to bake today, but I thought we could all get stuck into pizza.'

Or you can just look perfect and popular, when the rest of us get messy, Ivy thought sourly, as flour flaked off her hand on to the door handle.

But, no, she told herself, *that wasn't fair.* Olivia was right – Ivy was just overreacting to Holly . . . probably.

Even as she thought that, Holly leaned closer to peer at Ivy's face. 'You know what?' She laughed, but it sounded uncomfortable. 'I can't even tell which twin you are, under all that flour! Is that . . . is that Olivia?'

Ivy gritted her teeth. Clearly, Holly was really, *really* hoping it was Olivia. So much for giving each other a chance! 'You look nervous,' she snapped. 'Are you worried you might have to make conversation with a goth?'

'Ivy!'

Uh-oh. Ivy turned to find her twin standing right behind her, mouth open in shock.

Oh, great. Just what she needed! She'd left

Transylvania to escape all the watching eyes and strict codes of behaviour – but now that she was back in Franklin Grove, it was just as bad! Speaking her mind was somehow upsetting people.

What was the point of coming home at all? Ivy thought.

Deep down, she knew her anger really stemmed from guilt at her own bad behaviour. But right now, she didn't want to listen to the reasonable thoughts in her head. Instead, she turned on one heel and stalked back down the hallway to the kitchen.

'Here's Holly,' she said curtly to all the others, and then she went straight to a mixing station, turning her back to the group. Beating eggs really hard was strangely fun.

Behind her, her friends seemed to have turned themselves into the perkiest welcoming committee ever.

'Holly!' Sophia said warmly. 'Perfect timing.'

'Hey, it's good to see you again,' Brendan said. 'Is that pizza? Awesome.'

'We should talk!' said Camilla.

Ivy scowled down at her mixing bowl. *Has this girl cast a charm spell over everyone?* Or maybe Ivy's friends were just easily excited by pizza?

'It smells delicious,' Olivia said. 'What's in it, Holly?'

'Oh, you know . . .' Ivy could hear the smile in Holly's voice. 'A little bit of everything.'

'Ivy?' Olivia said. 'Do you want to cut the first slice?'

There was no polite way to refuse, not without everyone really thinking she was a monster. 'Fine,' Ivy growled, and took out a knife from the cutlery drawer.

At least Brendan was actually looking forward to eating something, for once. That was her only consolation.

The moment the pizza box opened, the smell seemed to rise out of it like a wild animal. It was so pungent and intense, Ivy could barely breathe. What in the world had Holly put in here? No matter what it was, Ivy would have to eat it and pretend to like it, just to keep Olivia happy. Gritting her teeth, Ivy sliced into the pizza . . . then almost gagged . . .

Oh no! This was even worse than she'd anticipated.

'Wow.' She fought to keep her voice bright, even as she tried not to inhale. 'Look everybody,' she said. 'Holly's stuffed the pizza-crust with *garlic*.'

Turning away, she slapped her hands to her face in a gesture of amazement, as a cover for the fact that she was blocking her mouth and nose. What was it about bunnies and *garlic*? Did they really have to put it on *everything*?

As Brendan and Sophia, the other vampires in the group, absorbed the news and tried not to retch, the room went dead silent. Ivy spotted Brendan turning to lean heavily over the sink. Oh no, just as she was trying to reinvigorate his love affair with food! Ivy dug her black-painted nails into the palms of her hands. *One more mark against Holly!*

Then her friends swung into action.

'You know what? I think I'll just open the window,' Sophia said. 'This summer heat is really getting to me.' Her tone was light, but Ivy saw her lean out the window as she opened it, taking deep, desperate breaths of air not contaminated by garlic.

At the same time, Brendan shifted to the other side of the room, raising one hand to his face, pretending to scratch just above his nose.

'You all really have to try this,' Holly said, oblivious to the panic. 'Honestly, it's great! I used my dad's recipe – that's why the crust is stuffed with garlic.'

Without waiting for any response, she took the knife from Ivy's hand and started cutting into the pizza, sending more whiffs of garlic into the air. 'Here, Ivy.' She held out a plate. 'You take the first slice.'

'Um . . . I think I hear the doorbell.' Ivy fled to the front door before she could do anything worse.

From a safe distance, she watched the others trying to avoid eating garlic – and not just the vampires. Camilla was human, but that didn't stop her from promptly slipping her piece into a houseplant pot. Brendan smiled through gritted teeth and made a big show of cutting his slice up into tiny portions – 'To make sure I savour every crumb of garlicky goodness' – before rushing into another room. Only Olivia was gamely eating two slices, trying to cover up for everyone else . . . but Ivy could have sworn she saw her twin's face turning green, even beneath the layer of Double-00 flour. Olivia might not be allergic to garlic, but Ivy knew she was hating every bite.

This was a nightmare – a Holly-shaped nightmare!

As Ivy stood holding open the front door, someone arrived – her dad! Ivy hadn't even known he'd slipped out. *He must have been running yet more wedding errands.*

'Oh good, pizza!' Charles said, hurrying past her towards the kitchen. 'Just what I need!'

'Dad, wait!' Ivy said. But it was too late. He was already accepting a slice from Holly, who beamed at his enthusiasm.

'Yum!' Charles said, and lifted it to his mouth. All the fresh air from the open windows must have wafted the scent of garlic away from him.

There was only one thing Ivy could do. She threw herself at her dad, full-body, and knocked the pizza out of his hand.

'It's garlic!' she whispered into his ear, too quietly for anyone else to hear. Then, as she straightened, she said loudly: 'Sorry about that. I guess I tripped.'

'Tripped?' Holly put her pizza box down, her smile drooping. Charles's slice of pizza lay on the floor between them, abandoned in the mass of flour, as he backed swiftly out of the room. Holly was still staring angrily at Ivy. 'From the *hallway*?'

'I'm sure that –' Olivia began.

'No, listen.' Holly jerked her chin up proudly. 'I know this was supposed to be a baking party, but I just wanted to try something different. I wasn't showing off, or being difficult – or whatever else Ivy thinks of me. I just thought it'd be fun. That's all. But I guess I was wrong. Ivy clearly doesn't want me here.'

'Holly, wait!' Olivia said.

But she brushed past her without a word.

Seconds later, the walls of the house shook as the front door slammed shut. Olivia swung around to face Ivy. 'Is Camilla still filming us?' she asked stiffly.

Ivy glanced around. 'Um, no. She's in the living room with the others – they all slipped out when things got . . . awkward.'

'Good.' Olivia shook her head. 'Because I need to tell you something, Ivy: you were really obnoxious to Holly! I know you had to avoid the garlic, but couldn't you have been polite about it?'

'*Polite?*' Ivy stared at her. 'What do you think I was supposed to do? Poison myself, just so I wouldn't hurt her feelings?'

Olivia crossed her arms. 'Did you *really* have to make such a big show of stopping Dad from eating that pizza? You actually threw yourself across the room to knock it out of his hands, right in front of her! What were you thinking?'

'You know I couldn't let Dad eat it,' Ivy said.

'Well, what happened to subtlety?' Olivia asked.

She's never been like this with me – ever, Ivy thought. A lump seemed to be forming in her throat, but she swallowed hard.

'Hey, guys?' Brendan stood in the doorway, looking awkward. 'The others are ready to go home now. I think your dad's a bit, um, twitchy about the mess.'

Olivia let out a groan, then turned to go play hostess.

As they all said their goodbyes, Ivy fought to hide the hurt brimming inside her. The whole time she'd been at Wallachia, she'd dreamed of coming home to be with her twin again. She'd assumed that Olivia would feel the same about having Ivy back.

It looks like I was wrong about that, she thought. A lot of things had changed while she was gone – like Olivia putting a stranger's feelings before Ivy's.

At last, the front door closed for the final time, leaving the twins on their own with Brendan to clear up the mess.

As he and Ivy knelt together to scrub the flour off the kitchen floor, he nudged her gently. 'Hey, it was a great party until the end, wasn't it?'

'I guess.' Ivy shrugged one shoulder.

'So why the deflated look?'

She just shook her head and scrubbed harder. She was afraid she would embarrass herself by crying if she tried to talk.

Olivia moved around them with a swish of her flour-covered apron. Ivy bit her lip and kept scrubbing.

Brendan sat back on his heels. 'You know,' he said gently to Olivia, 'you might have been embarrassed, but none of this was Ivy's fault – she was just trying to stop your dad from having a really bad allergic reaction.'

'I guess,' Olivia said eventually. Ivy wasn't

taking her eyes off the floor, but she could hear the shrug in her sister's voice. 'I just wish everyone could get along.'

'Me too,' Ivy said quietly.

She waited for Olivia to come and give her a hug, but instead she heard her twin wiping her hands, taking off her apron and heading into the living room without a word.

'Come on, Brendan.' Ivy pushed herself to her feet, ignoring the dull ache just below her throat. 'I'll see you to the door.'

When they were standing on the front step, she finally let herself lean into his shoulder. 'Olivia and I have never fallen out over another friend before,' she whispered.

'I know,' Brendan said. He wrapped his arms around her in a hug. 'But it'll be OK. You love her. She loves you. You'll get past it.'

'I hope so,' Ivy said, closing her eyes. 'Because this feels miserable.'

Chapter Four

That evening, Olivia sat next to Ivy at the dinner table, across from Charles and Lillian, with a dozen different trays of food between them. The two girls sat only a few centimetres apart. *So why does it feel as though there's a mile between us?* Olivia thought.

The room was shining clean, and now that everything had calmed down around the house, it seemed like the perfect time to talk to the vampire grown-ups about the mysterious blogger . . . if they could get a word in edgeways. And that wouldn't happen unless Ivy helped her out.

Ivy hadn't spoken a word to her in hours. By contrast, their bio-dad wouldn't stop talking.

'Now, don't forget to try the roasted red pepper in miniature taco shells,' Charles urged, pushing one of the trays forwards. In the entire year she'd known him, Olivia had never heard him talk so quickly. The combination of excitement and nerves was making her bio-dad as hyper as a honeybee. Lillian sat at his side, quietly nodding and murmuring encouraging words. *She's a saint!* Olivia thought. *A living, breathing saint.*

'Olivia, I know you can't have this one,' he continued, 'but Ivy, you must tell me what you think of the steak tartare! Then there are the blood-orange cocktails and the sugared almonds and . . .'

Olivia bit back a sigh as her dad continued. It was going to be a real challenge to get Charles's mind off the wedding and on to the blogger. She glanced at Ivy, trying to see if her twin was thinking the same thing, but Ivy's dark hair fell around her eyes.

It had taken a long time to get the house sparkling again after the party, but in the process of hard physical cleaning, Olivia had finally worked off most of her frustration. Yes, she still wished Ivy had handled the situation at the baking party differently, but . . . *It wasn't all Ivy's fault*. She could see that now. She really wanted to make up with her twin.

'Is everything all right?' Their dad's voice punctured the silence. Even he had finally picked up on the tension in the room. He looked between them, frowning. Lillian watched them both carefully, her eyes darting from Olivia's face to Ivy's. Olivia felt herself starting to blush. 'I know there are a lot of changes coming up for all of us, but I promise I'll still be your dad after the wedding. You don't have to worry about that.'

'It's OK,' Olivia said quietly. 'That's not it.'

'No, it isn't, is it?' Lillian asked.

Ivy shrugged silently.

Charles looked at his fiancée, then back at the girls. 'Oh, I get it. Would it help if you two were more involved in the wedding planning? Maybe –' his face lit up – 'you girls could write the names on the name plates for the table plans! That would make you feel better, wouldn't it?'

'Oh, Charles.' Lillian put one hand on his arm, shaking her head. 'Can't you see that the wedding is the last thing on the girls' minds?'

'What do you mean?' Charles blinked.

'How about, instead, we think about something more . . . hey! Check that out!' Leaning forwards, Lillian pointed out the window in an obvious attempt at distraction. 'Look at the clothes on that couple! How ridiculous!'

Olivia looked in the direction Lillian was pointing – and nearly choked as she saw the outrageously dressed elderly couple walking slowly up the hill towards Ivy's house. '*What* are they wearing?' They were the image of an over-the-top elderly couple on vacation – except that Franklin Grove hardly ever had appropriate weather for checked shorts, flowered shirts and sandals. One of them was wearing the most enormous sunglasses Olivia had ever seen. What on earth were they doing in Franklin Grove?

'Are they for real?' Ivy spluttered. 'Or do you think they got lost? Maybe they think they're still somewhere in Florida.'

Olivia laughed, loving that even Ivy couldn't keep up an Ice Queen act in the face of such a hilarious vision!

'It's almost as if they're *trying* to draw attention to themselves,' Lillian murmured.

Then Olivia stopped laughing as the couple turned up the path to Ivy's house, followed by another strangely dressed man.

'Wait a minute,' Ivy said, stiffening beside her. 'Isn't that . . .'

'Horatio!' Olivia breathed. She'd recognise the man's height and formal stance anywhere. It was the Lazar family's butler, which meant . . .

Charles actually rubbed his eyes once, then twice, as if to make sure he wasn't seeing things. 'Are those my parents?'

Olivia couldn't believe it, but he was right. The ludicrously dressed old couple were her grandparents, the Count and Countess Lazar!

The whole family rushed to let them in.

'Darlings!' The Countess opened her arms to her granddaughters as she stepped inside, somehow managing to look regal even in checked shorts. Olivia and Ivy both wrapped their arms round her and, for the first time in hours, their gazes met. It was only a brief, accidental glance, but Olivia felt just as warmed by her sister's softened expression as by her grandmother's arms.

'It's so good to see you,' the Countess said as she kissed Olivia's cheek.

'You too,' Olivia said. 'But what are you doing here?'

'And why are you wearing *bunny clothes*?' Ivy asked. From the look on her face, Olivia knew her twin had only barely managed to restrain herself from adding: *And such ridiculous ones?*

The Countess's bright-pink-and-orange flowered shirt was even more garish at close quarters. Olivia's eyes hurt just from looking at it. *Where are my diamante sunglasses?!*

'You must be here for the engagement party,' Charles exclaimed, as Horatio shut the door behind them. 'I'm afraid you are a bit early, but –'

Lillian shushed him. 'Why don't we wait for your parents to explain?'

'Of course we will explain,' the Countess said grandly. 'But first, I *must* change. These cheap polyesters make my skin itch!'

Then why are you wearing them? Olivia wondered. But she bit her tongue as her grandmother started to collect her luggage and head towards the stairs.

'No, no, no!' an outraged voice interrupted. Horatio swished past Olivia and in one smooth movement had collected the luggage from the Countess and tucked her cases under each arm. He lowered his gaze to the floor. 'So sorry. I didn't mean to be rude, but this is my job.' He started to walk up the stairs, turning awkwardly to avoid bumping the leather-bound luggage against the banisters. The Countess watched him, shaking her head indulgently.

'You know,' she whispered to Olivia. 'I haven't been allowed to carry a thing upstairs in over forty years.' Then she laughed quietly. 'But I do like to tease him and pretend I'm going to sometimes!'

Olivia was shocked. Had the Countess just . . . cracked a joke? Before she could dare to ask, her grandmother followed Horatio upstairs.

When she finally came back down, wearing her usual satin and cashmere, the entire family gathered in the living room, with the trays of wedding treats set in the centre of the room. Horatio circulated with a jug of iced tea. *How did he make that already? Wasn't he helping the Countess unpack?* Olivia wondered. The Countess sat in the place of honour in Charles's favourite chair. The Count was settled on the sofa, delicately nibbling a king prawn.

Charles and Lillian sat together. 'If you aren't here for the engagement party,' Charles said to his parents, 'what else could possibly have brought you?'

'We were sent by the Queen,' the Countess said, 'to investigate your daughters' message.'

'What message?' Charles turned to Olivia and Ivy, his brow creased. Olivia tried not to wince. *Uh-oh, here we go.*

74

'We did try to tell you,' Ivy said, 'but –'

The Countess cut across her. 'We all saw the twins' message on the Vorld Vide Veb about the vampire hunter. But what is all this about a "blagger" threatening to expose Franklin Grove's vampire community?'

Now Charles looked really shocked. 'A *what*?'

Horatio cleared his throat. 'Ahem. That would be "blogger", milady.'

Olivia bit the inside of her cheek to hold back a laugh at the disgruntled expression on her grandmother's face. The Countess clearly wasn't up to speed on the latest technology . . . which wasn't surprising, considering she was hundreds of years old.

'Blagger, blogger . . .' The Countess waved a hand through the air dismissively. 'Regardless, the Queen was alerted by her intertrap –'

'*Internet*,' Horatio interjected, in a whisper.

'Her Inter*net* security team that this bla–

this *blogger's* message is getting out of control. Something needs to be done! Obviously, some vampire seniority is needed at the heart of the danger, and as we have family here, it made sense for your father and I to be the ones sent on this fact-finding mission.'

'A fact-finding mission . . .' Charles repeated blankly, '. . . in Franklin Grove.'

The Count held out a tray to the Countess. 'Do try the sugared almonds, darling.'

'Oh, do you like them?' Obviously thrilled to be back in wedding territory, Charles beamed at his father. 'I thought perhaps after the ceremony –'

'Sugared almonds are not a priority!' The Countess raised her eyebrows warningly. 'We are here on an undercover mission of the greatest importance.'

Ivy choked. 'So . . . that's why you were dressed that way?'

'It was the only safe way to travel.' The Countess patted the Count's purple-and-yellow flowered shirt-sleeve with satisfaction. 'Our mission is to get the entire vampire community of Franklin Grove undercover until this threat has been neutralised. And, of course –' her expression hardened – 'no matter what it takes, we must discover the identity of the *blogger* who is responsible for stirring up so much trouble in the first place.'

Olivia gulped. 'Um . . . what exactly are you planning to do when you find it out?'

For the first time since their falling out, Ivy voluntarily made eye contact with Olivia. She drew a finger across her throat and let her eyes roll back in her head.

Olivia felt her heartbeat speeding up. Vampires wouldn't really go to such lengths to avenge themselves would they?

No, she thought. *Of course they wouldn't . . . right?*

She darted a glance at Charles and saw him staring hard at the floor, as if unable to meet her eyes.

Oh no, for real?

'Are you sure that isn't a bit, um, excessive?' she whispered.

'Well, I don't know, dear,' the Count said, clearing his throat noisily. 'We take these threats *very* seriously.' Olivia noticed that his shoulders were shaking as he turned his face away from her.

Was the Countess actually wiping a tear from her eye? Olivia swivelled back to look at Ivy, who was biting her knuckles with the effort of holding back laughter. Finally, a huge snort erupted from Charles as his whole body trembled with repressed chuckles.

'You're all pranking me!' Olivia was able to breathe again, a smile of relief spreading across her face. She grabbed a sofa cushion to swing at Ivy. 'It's not my fault! I don't know what vampire tradition is when it comes to this sort of thing!'

'Don't apologise, my dear. We enjoyed the joke.' The Countess patted Olivia's hand, her eyes still gleaming with amusement. 'But it is time to be serious once more. This intertrap – that is, this *Internet* person has drawn attention to Franklin Grove. Now the rumour is out about vampires living among humans in a normal American town – and do you know what that means?'

Charles let out a heartfelt groan. 'The VITs.'

Moans of unhappy agreement filled the room. Lillian closed her eyes as if she were in pain.

'Uh . . .' Meekly, Olivia put up her hand. 'What's a VIT?'

'A Vampire-Investigating Tourist.' Lillian shuddered as if she were naming an exotic kind of cockroach. 'Someone who gets wind of vampires' existence and travels across the country to check it out.'

'Oh.' Olivia's eyes widened. 'And now that the

blogger's told everybody that Franklin Grove is a haven for vamps –'

'We're going to see many more strangers in town,' Charles finished for her grimly. 'And they'll all be on the look-out.'

'Which is why Franklin Grove vampires must go undercover, just like us.' The Countess threw a pointed glance at Ivy's vamptastic dark clothes. 'Those will certainly have to be toned down!'

'Fine.' Ivy heaved a sigh. 'I can wear some of Olivia's clothes, I guess. No one will think I'm a vampire with all that pink!'

Olivia gave her a sympathetic smile. She knew how much Ivy would hate that disguise.

But the Countess was shaking her head. 'Absolutely not,' she declared. 'You mustn't change your appearance too drastically. Otherwise, the people who already know you well will start thinking something's wrong. And if the same people read that dreadful blag –'

Horatio cleared his throat, and the Countess scowled.

'*Blog!* They may put two and two together.' Clasping both hands around her glass of iced tea, she pinned Ivy with an eagle-like glare. 'You must be very, very careful about how you tone down your image. You're to become invisible.'

'Sorry?' Ivy choked on her iced tea. 'Grandma, you and Grandpa and Horatio are hardly subtle and toned down with *your* image!'

'Ah, but nobody really knows us in Franklin Grove. That means this isn't an image *change* — anyone who sees us will simply assume this is our normal dress-sense.' The Countess gestured with her iced tea at Horatio's bright-pink checked shorts, which revealed the dignified butler to have surprisingly knobbly knees.

Olivia stifled a giggle. It was certainly a dress-sense . . . but 'normal' was not the first word that came to mind!

Ivy rolled her eyes. 'Are you sure this is all really necessary? Making us all get bunnified just because of one blogger? Can't we just –'

'Ivy Vega.' The Countess's voice was suddenly as cold as ice, her hard gaze focused on her vampire granddaughter. 'Don't you think helping the local community is the least you can do after . . .?'

She let her last words drift off, but everyone knew what they would have been: after abandoning her studies in Transylvania. The Count and Countess obviously had not yet forgiven Ivy for leaving Wallachia.

Tradition meant everything to Olivia's and Ivy's grandparents, and as far as they were concerned, when Ivy had walked away from Wallachia, she had turned her back on tradition – and on them.

Olivia's heart melted at the misery on her sister's face. She put an arm around Ivy, hugging her close. 'Don't worry,' she said. 'We'll find out who the blogger is in no time. Then you can go right back to doing what you do best – being a totally fangtastic vampire!'

'*Fangtastic*?' Even Ivy had to smile at Olivia's weak joke. As laughter rippled through the room, Olivia felt relief flood her.

The tension between her and her sister had disappeared. At least, for a little while . . .

Chapter Five

This is unbelievable. Ivy lay in her coffin-bed early the next morning, listening to the noises of the house waking up. She was too depressed to even move. Yes, it was true that she had left Transylvania to stop feeling overwhelmed by all things vampire – but she had *never* expected that a return to Franklin Grove would leave her overwhelmed by all things bunny instead!

Nothing about coming home was turning out the way she'd expected.

A polite knock sounded on the door, and Ivy gave a rueful smile. At least some things never changed: no matter which house they were in, Horatio was always ready with a breakfast tray.

She climbed out of her coffin to let him in and noticed for the first time that Olivia's bed was empty. *That's weird.* Olivia had stayed the night to spend more time with their grandparents. Ivy had expected her to be fast asleep.

She was still frowning as she opened the door – but her jaw dropped when she saw what Horatio was wearing. Her gaze moved slowly, disbelievingly, from his high-top sneakers to his hooded jacket, his 'I'm With This Idiot' T-shirt and . . .

'Are you wearing *man-jewellery*?'

Blushing furiously, Horatio stuffed the wide, fake-gold chain under the neck of his T-shirt before leaning over the tray to pour tea into a china cup. 'It's the Countess's orders,' he explained stiffly, his cheeks beetroot red.

'Of course.' Ivy accepted the china cup,

forcing herself not to say another word. *Poor Horatio*, she thought, as he ducked out of the room. *I shouldn't make this even harder for him.*

But her sympathy evaporated a moment later when he returned, wheeling in a clothes rack. 'What is *that*?'

Horatio coughed apologetically. 'Your outfits for the day. Each item has been carefully selected for you by Miss Olivia.'

Wordlessly, Ivy picked up item after item, holding them between her fingertips and at arm's length. She didn't dare hold them any closer. It was too dangerous. *Just looking at them might give me Bunny-itis. Do I really have to wear them?*

'Good morning!' Olivia chirped from the bedroom doorway, as Horatio discreetly slipped out. 'Everything OK?'

'OK?' Ivy struggled not to give her twin a death-squint as she dropped the fashion monstrosities on to her bed. 'Just look at these!'

Seeing them all spread out together made her stomach twist with horror. For some reason, Olivia had given her a pink jersey ra-ra skirt, a colour-blocked emerald clutch bag to carry and a yellow lace T-shirt with pink ribbon ties on the sleeves.

Ivy moaned. 'Are you joking? Is this really my outfit for today?'

'Oh, Ivy. Don't be so silly.' Olivia rolled her eyes. 'I nearly forgot!' She reached into her pocket and pulled out an ostrich-feather hair slide. 'You wouldn't be dressed at all without the right accessories!'

Ivy felt the room swim around her. 'I honestly think I'm going to faint,' she whispered.

Olivia put one hand to her mouth, but she couldn't stifle her burst of giggles.

'I can't believe you're laughing!' Ivy could feel a supreme death-squint forming on her face as she watched Olivia slide down the wall to sit on the carpeted floor, still laughing. 'I know we had a fight yesterday, but how can you possibly think it's funny that I have to dress like *this*?'

'No, no, no.' Wiping away tears, Olivia shook her head. 'Don't worry! I *am* sorry about yesterday, but that has nothing to do with this. I was just playing a prank! You guys got me good yesterday, so I thought I'd have a little fun of my own today! Of course I'm not going to dress you up like an Olivia-clone . . . no matter how fabulous you'd look.'

'Don't even imagine it.' Ivy collapsed on to her own coffin-bed, crushing the pink skirt. She let out her breath in a rush. 'OK. OK, this can work. I'll just try to look a little less "gothabulous".'

'Well . . .' Olivia cupped her chin with a hand, and Ivy narrowed her eyes in suspicion. They might have forgiven each other for the day before, but right now she didn't trust Olivia's expression — not one bit. She looked just like one of those judgmental stylists on the kind of makeover shows that Ivy only watched when Olivia gave her a choice between that or helping with cheer-practice.

She crossed her arms. 'What are you thinking?'

'I'm sorry,' Olivia said, 'but if you want to be safe, we'll still need to abandon the goth look. No more pale face, no all-black ensembles . . .'

Ivy groaned, and pulled a pillow over her face.

'You know I'm right,' Olivia said. 'We can't give these VITs anything to be suspicious of. We just have to come up with a style shift that's subtle enough not to alert people who *already* know you that something's seriously different.'

'Easy peasy,' Ivy said, with an ironic tone of voice.

'Never fear,' Olivia smiled brightly. 'I have the perfect solution!'

Ivy watched with a feeling of mounting dread as Olivia jumped up and stepped into the hallway.

When she came back into the room, she was dragging a long sports bag behind her.

Don't panic, Ivy told herself. *She probably just needed a big bag. No way would Olivia actually expect me to . . .*

'Ta-da!' Olivia opened the bag and pulled out a pair of black trainers and sweatpants. 'How about this as a substitute? Sporty Ivy!'

Ivy couldn't stop herself from groaning. But she had to admit, at least it was better than the first outfit . . . and there was no holding back a cheerleader on a mission. Within minutes, Ivy found herself completely transformed by Olivia's 'disguise'. Her black hair was tied back in a high ponytail, and her grey T-shirt had a sports company logo emblazoned on it. Ivy couldn't even say which company it was – the name meant so little to her, she'd already forgotten it by the time she'd finished pulling the sleeves over her arms.

Or maybe she just wanted to pretend it wasn't really happening . . .

As she looked down at the outfit, she winced. *This has to be a bad dream.*

But Olivia looked absolutely thrilled. 'Am I a genius, or am I just a miracle worker?' Humming to herself, she bustled around Ivy, straightening her twin's ponytail and patting down the shoulders of Ivy's T-shirt. 'You see? It's still an alternative look, still all the same dark colours that people round Franklin Grove think of as "Ivy" – but, to anyone visiting . . .'

'Or *spying*,' Ivy muttered.

'. . . they'll simply think you're an ordinary tomboy.' Olivia stepped back, beaming. 'It's just right!'

'Are you joking?' Ivy kicked out her legs. 'Sweatpants are ridiculous when you're not actually *doing* any sport.' She wriggled miserably, feeling the way the baggy clothes fell around her. 'It's like being inside a sack.'

Olivia's raised her eyebrows. 'Well, think of it this way: if you need to run from any VITs, you'll be perfectly dressed for a quick getaway.'

Ivy's ponytail bounced against the back of her neck as she shook her head. 'I know you're trying to help, but this sucks . . . in the bad way! Just because some idiot blogger started up a rumour mill, I have to wear . . . *this*? I mean, honestly. Haven't I had to wear enough ridiculous outfits lately? After that awful school uniform . . .'

'Now, now.' Olivia gave her a sweet smile. 'Don't forget what I had to wear while you were at the Academy. Remember how I dressed up as a goth rocker girl to cover for you, just so Brendan and Sophia could go to that concert while you were gone?'

'Yeah, but you got to go to the Pall Bearers concert!'

'That,' Olivia said, 'was *not* a concert. It was a

full-on celebration of tuneless noise! So all's fair.'

Before Ivy could say another word, the door opened, and the Countess poked her head in.

'Are you all ready with your disguise?'

Ivy's gaze fixed on the bright yellow baseball hat on her usually elegant grandmother's head. She shook her head in disbelief. 'Oh, please!' She threw herself back into her coffin-bed. 'This is going too far.'

Ivy heard Olivia giggle, but there was no humour in their grandmother's expression as she stalked across the room.

'Now, I need you to listen to me, young lady. As one gets older, there comes a time to start thinking about what is best for others, not just for oneself. If you care about the vampire community, you *will* wear these clothes and blend in. Do you understand me? This is your chance to prove yourself to the community once and for all.'

Suddenly, Ivy's coffin-bed felt at least two sizes

too small. She'd known that her grandparents wouldn't truly understand why she needed to leave the Academy, but she had hoped they would accept it as her decision. *I only did what I thought was right. Isn't that the vampire way?*

Ivy didn't say anything in reply. She didn't even move when the Countess and Olivia quietly left the bedroom. What was the point, when it was looking like she didn't actually have a choice in any of this?

Only the sound of her cell phone ringing finally got her climbing out of the coffin-bed.

Brendan's voice was filled with amusement on the other end of the phone. 'Tell me the truth,' he said. 'What are you wearing?'

Ivy let out an unhappy half-laugh, settling cross-legged on the floor. 'You first,' she said.

'Well . . .' He coughed. Then he said, under his breath and so quickly she could barely understand him: 'A button-down shirt, chinos and loafers.'

94

'What?!' Ivy couldn't even imagine it. 'Are they making you dress like a middle-aged man?'

'That's not all,' Brendan said.

'Oh no,' said Ivy. 'Are you wearing a tie?'

'Worse,' he said. 'I have a side-parting.'

Ivy nearly dropped her cell phone. She recovered herself just in time to say, 'We're going to look like total opposites. I'm dressed like I'm forever on my way to the gym.'

When Brendan burst out laughing, Ivy finally started to see the funny side of her predicament. 'Fine,' she said. 'Laugh it up now. But we have to promise to keep straight faces when we actually see each other. Otherwise, that'll give the whole game away.'

'Got it,' Brendan said. 'Jock Ivy is totally normal. Yep, totally.'

Ivy grinned to herself. 'But the most important thing is, you can*not* actually *like* my new style. Understood? As soon as this little problem is cleared up, I am ditching this Jock look and going straight back to being me.'

'So . . .' Brendan said, sounding concerned. 'Does that mean I can't keep my side-parting?'

Ivy was feeling a whole lot better by the time she hung up and went downstairs, following the aroma of pancakes and blueberries to the kitchen. From the deliciousness of the smell, she knew exactly who to expect at the oven: Lillian.

When Ivy appeared in the kitchen, her future stepmom's mouth dropped open, and she had to fumble to keep from dropping her spatula. 'That's a little . . . different,' Lillian said, blinking hard.

'That's the whole point!' Olivia said. Finishing her last pancake, she dabbed neatly at her mouth with a napkin. '*Subtle* disguises,' she explained. 'Trust me, this is going to work.'

'Right,' Ivy said, doing her best to return Olivia's encouraging smile.

At least there's one consolation, she told herself. She might be dressed in a sack and advertising some sports company she couldn't care less about, but at least she and her twin were bonding again.

That was worth almost any disguise.

🦇 🦇 🦇

Olivia was just about to step through the doors of Franklin Grove mall that afternoon when a hand grabbed her arm and pulled her back.

'Ivy!' she gasped, as she ended up hidden behind the outer wall of the mall beside her twin. 'What's the matter with you? You and your vampire strength almost gave me whiplash!'

'The mall is full of VITs!' Ivy hissed.

'Oh no.' Olivia swallowed hard. 'They're here already?'

'Didn't you see the latest blog post?' Ivy's eyes looked wild. 'The title was: "Which mall is crawling with creatures of the night?"'

Olivia pulled free of her sister to peer through the glass doors. 'I don't see anything weird,' she said.

'Look closer.'

Olivia glanced inside. Teenagers gathered in groups at all the usual kiosks selling jewellery and toasted almonds, while more shoppers streamed out of the clothing stores carrying massive plastic bags. A trio of girls tried on pairs of sunglasses at the closest kiosk, while an older mother pushed a stroller past them. 'I still don't – *Oh.*'

Now that she looked closer, she could see that there was definitely something strange about the teenage couple sitting on a bench. For one thing, the newspaper they shared was upside-down . . . Then there was the girl by the food court wearing a long brown trench coat and a large crucifix necklace. Also . . .

Olivia's eyes narrowed. That girl outside the stationery store wasn't being nearly as subtle as she thought she was. She was taking cell-phone photos of everyone who passed her.

Ivy was right. This was not good. Franklin Grove's secret was under grave threat.

Olivia took a deep breath to settle her nerves. *Really*, she told herself. *Walking into a VIT-infested mall can't be harder than running out on to a football field to cheer in front of hundreds of spectators.*

'Ivy,' she said, 'if you can make it past these VITs, you will have passed the biggest test of your disguise.'

'Well . . . I guess that's true,' Ivy agreed, peering around Olivia's shoulder.

Olivia nodded firmly. 'Better yet, if we hang around the mall for a while, we might be able to find some clues to the blogger's identity. There must be some reason why the blogger told all those VITs to come here today.'

'You're right.' Ivy's eyes gleamed. 'I bet the blogger's somewhere in here too, hiding in the crowd. And he – or she – *so* needs to be taken down!'

Olivia pushed the mall doors open.

Showtime!

Together, they wandered through the mall, passing kiosks and shops on every side. Just as Olivia had hoped, none of the VITs paid them any attention. After all, why would they? She smiled smugly as she glanced at her sister's sweatpants and sporty T-shirt. There was nothing about Ivy to draw anyone's attention . . .

. . . until they passed a cookie stand in the food court that wafted the scent of fresh, delicious cookies through the air.

'*Bleagh!*' Ivy dry-heaved and retched so loudly that heads turned all around them.

'Hey!' The owner of the cookie stand looked hurt – and worried too, as he glanced at all the people watching. 'What's wrong with the smell of my cookies?'

'Nothing,' Ivy croaked. 'I just – *bleagh*!' She covered her mouth and nose.

Oh no, Olivia thought. *This is exactly the kind of attention Ivy doesn't need to attract!* Sure, some of their watchers were ordinary Franklin Grove locals, but others were definitely VITs . . . and they were watching the twins with narrowed eyes. Why would a normal teenage girl retch at the aroma of sugar? Olivia wasn't sure herself – Ivy didn't usually have a problem with sweet snacks. She knew what everyone must be thinking as they stared at Ivy. Maybe this normal teenage girl isn't so normal . . . *We have to get out of here – fast.*

Olivia wrapped her arm around Ivy, even though she had no idea what was causing her twin's reaction. 'I'm sure it's not your cookies,' she reassured the stand owner, as she started to steer Ivy away. 'They smell delicious. Now we'll just get out of your way and –'

'They don't smell delicious, they *are* delicious.'

The cookie maker glared at Ivy. 'Here, try one! Take it!' He scooped out a cookie and waved it at her. 'Just eat one of my cookies and then tell me how the smell could make you sick!'

'I can't – sorry, I – *bleagh*!' As Ivy broke off to dry-heave, Olivia led her away from the stand owner, who still held his cookie aloft, yelling after them that they should *really* try one. She could feel the suspicious stares of the VITs following them all the way through the food court.

One VIT even stood up as they passed his table, waving a strange, ropy necklace at them in a motion that almost looked threatening. 'Hey! Is something making you ill?'

Olivia glared at him. Did he have to sound so hopeful? And why was he waving his jewellery at them? She didn't have time to stop and look closely at his strange necklace, not with Ivy bent over, green-faced and looking ready to throw up at any moment. 'We're fine!' she snapped.

102

'We just need a bit of privacy.'

She had never been so relieved to leave the food court in her life. As soon as they were well out of range, she pulled her twin into a hidden alcove between two stores.

'What's wrong? Those cookies smelled amazing.'

'It wasn't the cookies.' Gasping for breath, Ivy shook her head. 'It's garlic. I can smell garlic *everywhere*!'

'Really?' Frowning, Olivia peeped out from their alcove . . . and sucked in a breath as she suddenly understood.

All the VITs walking past were wearing long coats and jackets – long enough for hiding things inside . . . and, as the two closest VITs walked past, Olivia could see crudely made chains of garlic wrapped around their necks.

That was what had been on the other VIT's necklace: garlic! That must be why the VITs were here today: to root out vampires, using garlic like a dowsing rod. *Oh no!* Olivia paled as she finally made the connection. *That* was why the VIT in the food court had waved his necklace right at Ivy — and why he'd sounded so hopeful when he'd asked if she was ill.

And now they'll all know that it worked.

Suddenly, Olivia felt ill too. The mall was full of garlic-carrying vampire hunters, who'd already managed to target her twin sister . . .

. . . and the vampires of Franklin Grove were in even more danger than she'd realised.

Chapter Six

It took another few minutes before Ivy started to get her breath back. As soon as she did, though, she said: 'We have to stay in the mall.'

Olivia stared at her. 'Are you crazy? This place is full of garlic. Those VITs already saw you get ill from the smell –'

'And that's exactly why I can't run away.' Ivy squared her shoulders. 'If I leave now, it'll prove to them that they were right. I *have* to stay and act normal, so they'll think that they just made a mistake.'

'But how can you?' Olivia shook her head. 'With all this garlic –'

'Come on,' Ivy said. She grinned ruefully. 'Just this once, you can drag me to the perfume counters. By the time I let those saleswomen spritz me with all their stinky samples, I won't be able to smell a thing.'

'If you're sure . . .' Biting her lip, Olivia stepped out of the alcove, heading with Ivy towards the closest department store. When they passed a crowd of VITs with their coats open over their garlic necklaces, she gave Ivy's arm a supportive squeeze. Ivy smiled as though everything was normal, and the VITs looked away, disappointed.

Olivia had never been so proud of her twin before. *Ivy really is the strongest person I know.*

She was so proud, she barely even let herself smile at the sight of Ivy grimacing as she allowed herself to be sprayed with samples of almost every perfume the department store had in stock. By the time the store assistants were finished, even Olivia's nose was feeling numb!

But it was worth it. When they passed another crowd of VITs on their way out of the department store, Ivy sailed past them without a twinge. 'It should *not* just be vamps that hate garlic,' Ivy mumbled. 'How can anyone actually enjoy something that smells like *that*?'

Ivy continued ranting, but Olivia was distracted by the sight of a book-signing going on in the bookstore ahead of them. Wistfulness pricked her. The last time she'd been here for a signing, it had been when Jackson was autographing copies of *Jackson's Journal*. If she half closed her eyes, she could still see him sitting there at the front table, his blond hair gleaming in the store lights as he smiled straight at her . . .

No, Olivia told herself firmly. She was over Jackson. *Over, over, over.* And – she checked out the poster – this was definitely not Jackson's signing. No, this author was called S. K. Reardon, and . . .

. . . *No way!* S. K. Reardon was the author of *Bare Throats at Sunset.* Holly would love this!

Olivia reached into her bag to grab her cell phone. 'I've got to let Holly know who's here,' she said, cutting across Ivy's garlic rant. She pointed in the direction of the bookstore. 'Look – it's that author Holly's always going on about. I can't wait to hear her reaction!'

'Wait a minute!' Ivy put out a hand to stop her before she could press a single key on the phone. 'What are you doing? We're on a mission. We can't have any old bunny tagging along for the ride!'

'Come on, Ivy.' Olivia sighed. 'We can at least let Holly know her favourite author is in Franklin Grove. Don't you even *want* to make amends for the pizza incident?'

Ivy scowled. 'If this is Holly's favourite author, she'd already know where he's appearing. Otherwise, what sort of fan is she?'

'Oh, not this again.' Olivia gritted her teeth.

'All I'm saying –'

'Don't,' Olivia pleaded. 'Just don't say anything mean about her, OK? She's the one person who stopped me from feeling completely lonely and miserable after you went off to the Academy. Doesn't that mean anything to you?'

Ivy's shoulders hunched. 'I couldn't help going to the Academy.'

'I know, but that doesn't change what happened, for either of us.' Olivia pulled her hand free. 'Now, come on. We can at least let Holly know about the signing, so she and I can take some photos together. It'll be really nice for her.'

'But what am I supposed to do while you're off playing fan-girl with Holly?' Ivy asked. 'Considering that I hate the book *and* I don't have a camera with me?'

Olivia shrugged, scrolling through her cell phone's address book to find Holly's number.

'Maybe you can . . . erm . . . look for more clues?'

'Oh, great.' Ivy rolled her eyes, but Olivia could see the amusement in her face. 'Good excuse, sis. *I* see what's happening. You're off to have fun while I do all the real work, huh?'

'It's not like that!' Olivia said. 'I just want to do something nice for Holly, since she's been feeling so left out. You'd be so good, with your flair for investigation.'

'All right, all right,' said Ivy, and nudged Olivia teasingly. 'You know flattery always works on me. Call Holly.'

'Thank you,' Olivia said, flashing her sunniest smile.

Ivy might act the big grump, but Olivia knew that if she could just talk her sister into letting down her guard, she could finally persuade her to see Holly's good side – and no one was more loyal than Ivy once she'd accepted a new friend. Olivia was determined to make that happen. Even if they did have undercover bloggers to track down, there was no reason why they couldn't be nice to Holly at the same time.

She looked at her phone – then scowled. 'Oh no! The reception here is terrible.' She waved it in the air hopefully, but nothing worked. 'Drat! I need to go outside to make the call. Do you want to come?'

'Are you kidding?' Ivy was already starting for the door, looking like she'd just won the lottery. 'I would *pay* to get some fresh air right now!'

As they stepped outside into the sunlight, Ivy took a deep, long breath. 'Ohhh, that's better . . . Hey, wait a minute.' Her eyes narrowed, and she pointed across the street. 'Is that our grandparents?'

Olivia shaded her eyes and looked in the direction of Ivy's pointing finger. 'Uh-oh.'

The brightly dressed couple was definitely the Count and Countess in full-on bunny disguise . . .

and they were tearing posters for *Bare Throats at Sunset* from shop windows and telephone poles all along the street. Their enormous Florida-style sunglasses made them look even more suspicious as they glanced shiftily up and down the street before ripping down each new poster and tucking it under their arms.

'Um . . . should they be doing that?' Olivia asked.

'Those posters *are* covered in pictures of vampires,' Ivy said doubtfully. 'And the less focus on vamps in Franklin Grove, the better . . . but you're right. I really don't think it's a good idea.' She sighed. 'Will you come with me to talk to them? I don't think they're in the mood to listen to me about anything right now.'

Olivia gave her twin a sympathetic smile and slipped her phone back into her shoulder bag. 'Of course,' she said. 'Let's go.'

The twins crossed the street together, and

were greeted by bright smiles from both of their grandparents.

'What excellent timing,' the Countess said. 'You can help us hunt down all the rest of these posters!'

'Grandma . . .' Ivy began. She looked uncomfortable, and Olivia knew that she was dreading another argument.

Quickly, she said, 'Why don't you leave those posters in place, Grandma? Actually, why don't you come to the book-signing yourselves? It'll give you a good clue to who's vampire-mad in town.'

'That's right,' Ivy said, brightening. 'It could work like a trap, to draw them in. And you never know – one of the book fans might even be the blogger.'

'My goodness,' the Countess said. She exchanged a glance with the Count. 'That is an excellent idea!'

Ivy glowed at the praise, and the Count beamed down at both of his granddaughters, dropping his stack of posters into a nearby bin. 'Obviously, you girls have inherited your detective skills from my side of the family.'

'I beg your pardon?' The Countess raised her eyebrows. 'Do I have to remind you that it was *my* family line that included Giovanni, the famous Vampire Investigator of old?'

'Now, now, my dear.' The Count's eyes glinted with mischief as he baited his wife. 'You can hardly claim a *nineteenth* cousin!'

Olivia stepped aside to make her phone call, but she was so drawn into watching the humorous bickering between her grandparents that she barely noticed that Holly's phone had gone to voicemail. 'Holly, this is . . . oops.' A beep sounded, signalling that she'd been cut off.

Never mind, I'll just send her a text.

She typed it in quickly, as Ivy warned their

grandparents about the garlic issue in the mall.

'If you want to stay out here to keep safe . . . .' Ivy began.

'Absolutely not.' The Count set his jaw proudly. 'Now that we've been warned, I can take it.'

'And I came prepared for every eventuality,' said the Countess. She reached into the pocket of her green-and-orange golfing trousers and pulled out a tiny bottle of Chanel No. 5. 'There!' She spritzed a cloud around her neck and hair. 'Safely shielded.' She gave the Count a stern look. 'And I warn you, dear, if you make any more claims about your great-aunt Helga, I'll spray you with it, too!'

The Count and Countess were still bickering over ancient family history when they reached the bookstore. S. K. Reardon – a tallish man with a mop of blond hair – sat at the front table holding a gold pen ready to sign his books.

Unfortunately, Olivia could see that there was

no queue of eager readers waiting to have their books signed, the way there had been at Jackson's event. *There are hardly any customers in the shop at all! Poor man*, Olivia thought.

As she stepped inside, her eyes locked with Reardon's for an awkward moment. Desperate hope flashed across his face. He lifted his pen in anticipation.

Oh no, Olivia thought. 'Quickly!' she mumbled to the others. 'Pick up a book, pick up a book!'

'What? Oh, yes. Of course.' The Count quickly scooped up a copy of *Bare Throats at Sunset* from the towering – and previously untouched – pile at the front of the store. 'Er.' He coughed and hurried towards the table, where S. K. Reardon was watching them intensely. 'Would you mind?'

'Of course not! I'd be delighted.' Reardon snatched the book from his hands before the Count could even finish his request. 'I hope you enjoy . . .' His words trailed off as he looked up and found the Countess giving him a death-glare from over the Count's shoulder. The author's pen froze before it even reached the page.

She looked him up and down with obvious disdain, and he visibly gulped, the pen sliding out of his grip. 'Ah, can I help you with anything else?'

'Just tell me this, S. K.,' the Countess said icily, as the Count picked the unsigned book back up and began to flip through the opening pages. 'Do you happen to have a *blag*?'

Oh no, Olivia thought. She wanted to do something, but she was frozen with horror. Ivy had already moved away, circulating through the shop with a watchful gaze.

'An, erm, what?' The author looked confused.

'You know!' The Countess waved one hand impatiently, nearly hitting him on the nose. 'Are you a blagger?'

S. K. Reardon stiffened in outrage. 'I have

been called many things, madam, but a *blagger* is not one of them!'

'Hmmph.' The Countess sniffed. 'Well, I suppose you're no real danger, then.'

'Excuse me?' He stared at her.

'I wish you well with your little . . . book,' the Countess said stiffly, turning away.

She bumped into the Count, who had been completely absorbed by the novel. With his vampire speed-reading, he had nearly finished the whole thing. 'I say!' He looked up at the author, wide-eyed. 'This book is fantastic!'

'It is?' S. K. brightened, looking pathetically hopeful.

'It really is! Although of course no *real* vampire would –'

'Grandpa!' Olivia finally managed to find her voice. She scooted over and took the book from him. 'Don't you want to get it signed?'

'Of course, of course.' The Count smiled

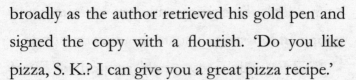

broadly as the author retrieved his gold pen and signed the copy with a flourish. 'Do you like pizza, S. K.? I can give you a great pizza recipe.'

Olivia couldn't believe it. She knew the Count adored pizza, but offering to share recipes with an author? This book really must be something special.

'Er . . . thank you.' S. K. looked even more confused now. 'I actually have a recipe of my own I like. But thank you . . . both . . . for your attention.' He loosened his collar, perspiring as the Countess sent him another icy glare.

Olivia mouthed to Ivy across the store. '*Help!*'

'Come on, Grandma,' Ivy said, hurrying back to them. 'Let's go.'

Just as they moved away from the signing desk, a huge crowd of excited VITs burst into the bookstore.

'Look!' the first one yelled. 'There's the vampire author!'

119

Suddenly the signing table was surrounded by people in long trench coats shouting questions.

'Did Franklin Grove really inspire *Bare Throats at Sunset*?'

'Is it true that you based the lake scene on the local duck pond?'

'How did you *know* about the secret of Franklin Grove?' a girl gasped, fluttering her eyelashes at him.

One man clutched a copy of *Bare Throats at Sunset* to his trench coat. 'Will this book really reveal the "secrets of the shadows"?'

'I'm sorry?' S. K. Reardon looked bewildered. 'I have no idea what you're talking about!'

Hmm, Olivia thought. Maybe she was just being naïve, but she believed him. He looked as stunned by the sudden attention as if a truck had just ploughed into him. He certainly didn't look prepared for any of the questions being shouted at him.

'I don't – I mean, I don't know where you heard any of that, but –'

'Oh! Of course. You mean we shouldn't be talking about it here in public.' One of the men who'd been shouting questions stopped and looked over his shoulder anxiously, scanning the room. He dropped his voice to a stage whisper. 'You're right, we have to be careful. After all, *they* could be anywhere!'

He threw Ivy a quick glance, taking in her sweatpants and sneakers. Then he shrugged, turning back with an embarrassed look. 'Or, well, you know, maybe the threat isn't *so* immediate. But still! They could be in one of the other stores.'

Ha! Olivia had to cover her mouth to hold back her laughter, even as S. K. Reardon shook his head in open disbelief.

The author looked as if he thought everyone around him had gone crazy, but Olivia was thrilled by the VIT's reaction. Ivy's disguise was certainly working – no one would take her for a vamp in a million years! Right now, Olivia's twin looked like nothing more than a regular tomboy. She wasn't in danger of discovery at the moment . . . but the mystery was getting more complicated than ever.

'What are all these people doing here?' Ivy muttered, as they shifted back to accommodate the last few VITs crowding into the store. Despite her perfume shield, her cheeks were starting to turn slightly green from the intensity of the garlic stench trapped in the store. 'I thought they were all busy trying to track down vampires with their ropes of garlic? Why should they care about an author signing?'

'It *is* odd that so many of them turned up at the same time,' Olivia agreed.

'Obviously they've all been reading the blagger,' said the Countess, gazing speculatively at the circle of trench coats. 'So maybe that scoundrel is behind this too.'

'I guess it is a nice coincidence for this author that a load of vampire fanatics happen to be in town when he's here promoting his novel.' Olivia shrugged. 'Do you think the two events are linked?'

Ivy was frowning hard now. 'Could be . . . It would certainly help explain why this mystery blogger highlighted the mall.' She turned to Olivia. 'Perhaps there's more to this than meets the eye.'

Olivia stood on tiptoes to peer through the crowd. S. K. Reardon was surrounded by VITs, but she couldn't see any sign of the biggest fan she knew: Holly. Maybe she still hadn't gotten the text. *I need to try again*, Olivia thought. If Holly could infiltrate the queue of VITs, she might be able to overhear something. Of course, Olivia couldn't share the vampire secret with Holly, but it wouldn't hurt to ask a few innocent questions about anything her friend might have picked up from the crowd of book-buyers. *You never know. It might work.*

'I'll be right back,' Olivia said. Ivy nodded, but neither of their grandparents bothered to reply. The Countess was busy watching the VITs with a raptor's predatory gaze, while the Count was re-reading *Bare Throats at Sunset* and happily murmuring to himself as he read.

Olivia just caught the words, 'Now what *I'd* do if that happened . . .' as she slipped past him on her way out of the store.

At least S. K. had gained one *real* vampire fan!

Once Olivia was outside the mall again, with a working signal, a beep sounded on her phone almost immediately. It was a text from Holly, sent only a minute earlier:

Oooh, I might be too shy. I'll think about it . . .

She'd obviously received Olivia's text about the signing. But, Holly – shy? This was the girl who'd stood up to Garrick in front of all the

Beasts, telling him to go home and take a shower!

Olivia sighed. Maybe big crowds *were* scarier than the Beasts. Or maybe Holly was just wary about being around Ivy after the baking party that would almost certainly go down in Franklin Grove history as 'Garlic Day'.

Her shoulders slumped. Oh well, it looked as though she wouldn't be able to get Holly in amongst the VITs. But worse than that – how was she supposed to prove to Holly and Ivy that they ought to be friends if they never hung out together again?

She headed back into the mall to find Ivy waiting for her in the bookstore. Ivy glanced at the phone in her hand.

'Problems?' she asked.

She probably thinks it's another call from Jackson, Olivia thought.

'Oh, it's nothing, really. I texted Holly to let her know her favourite author is in the mall but she thinks she's too shy to come and see him.'

Ivy rolled her eyes. 'Whatever. Come on, let's do some more clue hunting.'

But as they walked through the aisles of the crowded bookstore, Olivia caught sight of a corner of a hippy flower appliqué on a pair of jeans. Was that . . . could that be *Holly*?

Suddenly, there was the flash of a camera. She turned towards the source and spotted Holly in the corner of the bookstore photographing S. K. Reardon and all the VITs waiting to have their books signed.

But she said she was too shy to come down! Olivia stared, trying to understand. The text had only been sent a few minutes ago, and it had definitely made it seem like Holly was still at home – but here she was! No way could she have made the trip to the mall in the past few minutes. *Why would she lie to me?*

As she watched, S. K. spotted Holly. His

mouth dropped open. Then he pushed his chair back and headed straight towards her.

Oh, wow, Olivia thought. *Holly will be thrilled!* Her favourite author had recognised her. *She must have been to his signings before.*

Holly looked anything *but* thrilled, though. Her eyes widened, then she ducked her head and edged away. She wasn't fast enough to avoid the author. As he reached her, she started talking fast. Olivia couldn't catch any of the words, but Holly's expression was pleading.

S. K., on the other hand, looked furious. As he lectured her, his voice rose until Olivia could hear him from across the store:

'You can't do this! You're making things up!' He was almost shouting.

'Well, so do you!' Holly cried back. Then she seemed to catch herself, glancing nervously over her shoulder.

Olivia ducked out of sight, pulling Ivy with her.

The expression on her sister's face was grim. 'Can you believe that?' Ivy asked, nodding towards Holly.

Olivia gulped. *This is not how today was supposed to go.* Her new friend was fibbing to her, Olivia and Ivy were hiding . . . and her twin's growing mistrust of Holly had just hardened into stone.

Worse yet, for the very first time, Olivia found herself wondering whether there was any small chance that Ivy might actually be right about her new friend.

No, she told herself. *There has to be an explanation!*

But as she watched Holly storm out of the bookstore, straight into the neighbouring Internet café, she couldn't think of a single explanation that would work.

Chapter Seven

'Perfect.' Ivy nudged Olivia in the ribs as they watched Holly settle down at a computer terminal. Almost immediately, Holly started typing furiously – almost as if she were updating something. Could it be . . . *a blog*? 'She's on her own now. Let's go ask her what she's up to.' *And see exactly what she's typing!* Ivy thought to herself.

But her twin looked utterly miserable. 'We can't,' Olivia said. 'Didn't you see how upset she was? I think we should give her some space. When she's ready, she might tell us what happened. I'm sure there's a perfectly reasonable explanation.'

Olivia looked as though she was about to burst into tears. Ivy could tell that she knew Holly was behaving strangely, but that she couldn't bear to admit it. But all of a sudden, Holly was looking like a serious candidate for their mystery blogger.

I can't believe I've been so slow. Ivy dared a glance at her sister. *But I can't tell Olivia. Not yet.* Her twin had been so impressed by Holly. Now she looked so disappointed, just because Holly had told her one lie. Ivy could only imagine how badly Olivia would react to the suggestion that Holly might actually be the blogger who'd caused the vampires so much trouble. It could turn into the biggest fight they'd ever had.

No, Ivy would need real proof before she let Olivia even suspect what she was thinking. In the meantime, though . . . *Olivia is smart*, Ivy thought. *All I have to do is encourage her to follow the clues that she's been ignoring. She'll figure out the rest of it herself — and then we won't have to fight about it!*

'You're right,' she said. 'We shouldn't bother Holly right now. Do you have your netbook on you? There might be some fun things to look at soon. You know, if Holly has photos to share.'

'Oh! That's a good idea.' Olivia practically glowed with relief. 'I bet Holly's uploading her snaps of the book-signing right now! She's always putting up her photos on some social networking site.' She sat down on a bench and unzipped her shoulder bag. 'If we take a good look at her pictures, we might find some clues to the mystery blogger. There might be a stranger lurking in the background of a shot, or something like that!'

Ivy had to restrain herself from rolling her eyes. How could Olivia be so determined to miss the obvious?

She plopped down on the bench beside Olivia. 'What is going on?' she groaned dramatically. 'Why are so many people convinced that book was inspired by real vampires here in Franklin Grove?'

'It is strange,' Olivia agreed. 'You guys have lived in secret all these years without attracting any trouble.'

'So what could have gone wrong?' Ivy said. 'What could have *changed*?'

She looked meaningfully at her sister, willing her to think it through . . . to ask herself who the newest person in town was, the one whose arrival had just *happened* to coincide with the blog.

But Olivia was busy sliding her netbook out of her bag. 'Come on,' she said. 'Let's go sit in a café. It'll be easier to work on a table.'

Ivy followed, biting back her frustration. It wasn't until they'd ordered their drinks and sat down that Olivia finally answered her question.

'I don't know,' she said, and shrugged, her large eyes clear and innocent. 'I have no idea what could have changed. It's a mystery.'

Oh, come on! The truth was right there in front of Olivia's face, but she was refusing to see it.

'Here it is,' Olivia said brightly, leaning over her netbook. 'Holly's social networking profile.'

'Let's see.' Ivy leaned over her twin's shoulder.

Sure enough, Holly had been uploading photos on her profile page, along with lots of plugs for the book-signing.

'Look!' Olivia gasped. 'Even Holly's heard about the blog – she's linked her captions to it! The vampire hunter – whoever it is – must be going viral.'

Ivy raised her eyebrows and tried to trade a look with Olivia, but her twin didn't meet her gaze.

Biting her lip, Olivia clicked through the link to the blog without a word.

'Oh no,' Ivy moaned. 'What a nightmare!'

Now the blogger was asking for tips to flush out vampires! Worse yet, people all over the world had responded with their suggestions. Some of them were ridiculous . . .

'*Rope a giant wooden cross to your car roof,*' Ivy read out loud in disbelief, '*and vampires will dive for cover!* Are these people serious?'

But there were other tips too close to the truth to be ignored.

Olivia's voice was a bare thread of a whisper as she read the worst out loud: '*Mix garlic paste in your ice-cream and make everyone sundaes – your vampire enemy will faint!*'

'Ouch.' Ivy swallowed hard. 'At least they're not all spot-on. Check out this one – *See who looks most ridiculous wearing fake tan – sure to be a vampire!* Honestly.' She rolled her eyes. 'There sure are some idiots out there.'

'They're not all idiots,' Olivia said, scrolling down the list of suggestions. She was looking almost as pale as Ivy now. 'Some of these could really work.'

'Maybe,' said Ivy, 'but Holly has done us a favour by leading us here. Just look – the vampire-blogger wants all these tips for an exposé they're planning tonight. This means the blogger is in Franklin Grove mall *right this minute.*'

'Really?' Olivia's mouth dropped open. 'How do you know that?'

Ivy couldn't stop herself from grinning as she pointed at the corner of the screen. 'Look here, silly.'

'Oh.' Olivia flushed. 'A "Where Am I?" app . . .'

'. . . Showing us all exactly where they are on an interactive map,' Ivy finished with satisfaction. 'And the blogger is in the mall right now!'

Sitting back, Ivy watched as Olivia took a deep breath, staring at the screen with a horrified expression. *Finally*, Ivy thought. Was the penny dropping for Olivia? The blogger was in the mall and Holly was online – how much more obvious could it be?

As the silence stretched out, Ivy frowned. If Olivia had finally caught on, why wasn't she saying anything? She couldn't actually be trying to *protect* Holly, could she? A chill crept through Ivy at the thought. Would Olivia really choose this girl over the safety of her own family?

No. Ivy shook that thought away. Olivia would never betray Ivy and their bio-dad – not to mention their other friends. She waited and waited, her foot jiggling.

I can't take it any more!

'Right, that's it. I'm taking things into my own hands,' Ivy announced, and took the netbook from her twin. 'If any fool can post a ridiculous tip about flushing out vampires, so can I.'

'Uh-oh!' Olivia gasped. 'What are you doing?'

'Making that blogger's day.' Ivy grinned as she set up an instant message session with the blogger, via a link in the blog's sidebar. 'Let's see, I'll call myself . . . how about Van Helsing? Or Dracula-Hunter?'

'How about "insane"?' Olivia suggested.

Then both girls jumped as the screen beeped. The blogger had responded to Ivy's message.

Excitement shot through Ivy's veins as she hunched over the netbook. *'Franklin Grove isn't the first town I've visited with vampires,'* she typed. *'But I've already found out something astonishing about the local vampire community.'*

The blogger's response was immediate: *'Share your info, Dracula-Hunter!'*

'Sis . . .' Olivia began warningly.

Ivy ignored her. *'It's too private to share online,'* she typed. *'But if you meet me at the Franklin Grove graveyard tonight, I'll tell you everything in person.'*

'Ivy!' Olivia yelped.

The blogger had already responded: *'I'll see you there at midnight.'*

Ivy glanced across the mall at Holly. She

137

was smiling, as though she had just learned a new secret. Bingo. Ivy closed down the instant messenger, feeling smug. Across the mall, she glimpsed Holly standing up from her computer. 'Am I good, or what?' she asked Olivia. *If this doesn't flush Holly out, nothing will.*

'You can't do that!' Olivia shook her head frantically, although she had no idea Ivy had just set a date with Holly. 'Ivy, you could be putting yourself in serious danger. This person really does *not* like vampires, remember?'

'Who do you think this person is?' Ivy challenged.

Olivia's glance fell to the floor, and Ivy grimaced. *All right, then. I'll have to do it the hard way.*

She folded her arms. 'This blogger's nothing more than a bully, and I'm tired of letting her – or him – intimidate everyone in town. I want to flush this person out – whoever it is.'

'But for all you know, the blogger could

actually try to *hurt* you. Didn't you read some of those tips?'

'Do you really think –' Ivy snorted, but she stopped herself just in time. She'd been about to ask Olivia if she really thought Holly was capable of hurting her. But it was clear that Olivia wasn't ready to admit the truth about the blogger's identity. Ivy would just have to put Holly in the picture once and for all – tonight in the Franklin Grove graveyard! 'I'm not about to let some bunny with a blog hurt me. No, I'm going to meet her – or him – tonight, no matter what. Are you in or out?'

Olivia shook her head. 'I'm sorry, Ivy, but no way am I in. It's just too dangerous.'

'Oh, come on,' Ivy began. 'If we have a real chance of exposing the blogger, what does a bit of danger matter?'

Olivia swallowed hard. 'I'm sorry, Ivy. It's not worth it.'

'Not worth it?' Ivy got stiffly to her feet, shaking out her baggy black sweatpants. 'Don't you even care that the entire vampire community is at risk? Or is that just one more thing that changed for you while I was gone?'

'Ivy . . .' Olivia began, looking down at her hands.

'Forget it,' Ivy said. Hurt clogged her throat as she stepped away from the table. 'Obviously you've changed too.'

As she stalked past on her way out of the mall, her furious glare landed on Holly, who was leaving the Internet café. *That girl!*

Ivy had always loved Olivia's good and open nature. But now it felt as though her sister's willingness to believe the best of people had brought a genuinely dangerous person into the vampire community's path.

She pushed her way through the crowd of VITs and finally burst through the front door of the mall, sucking in deep breaths of non-garlic-tainted air.

Focus, she told herself. Her stomach might be roiling with hurt and anger and confusion, but she knew one thing for sure.

She couldn't throw any accusations or theories around until she had absolute proof that she was right, and the only way to get that proof was to attend tonight's meeting in the graveyard – no matter how dangerous it might be. Her relationship with Olivia – the most important in her life – might just depend on it.

🦇   🦇   🦇

An hour later, Olivia sat alone at the Meat and Greet, feeling not just lonely but exposed in her booth by the window. For once, the restaurant was almost completely empty. The only other customers there were a few regular humans, who looked baffled by the deserted booths surrounding them. Olivia knew the local vamps were staying away because of the blog. Too many pale-faced people in a meat-lover's restaurant – wearing dark clothes and eating *very* rare burgers – would definitely look suspicious. But she felt bad for the staff here, who looked nervous and unsettled by the sudden lack of business.

But then, Olivia thought, *when haven't I felt bad lately*? In fact, she realised that right now she felt completely miserable. Not only was the atmosphere in Franklin Grove crackling with tension, but she and Ivy hadn't stopped bickering ever since Ivy had returned from Transylvania.

The bell on the door jingled, and Olivia sighed with relief as she saw Brendan come in, dressed in a button-down shirt and chinos. She'd only sent the text to him five minutes ago – even at vampire speed, he'd gotten here earlier than she'd expected. He must have been worried too.

'Don't you dare laugh at what I'm wearing,'

he warned as he slid into the booth across from her. In his stiff button-down shirt, he looked as awkward as a little boy wearing his father's clothes.

Biting the inside of her cheek, Olivia just smiled.

'I know, I look ridiculous.' Brendan sighed, took a quick glance around the nearly empty restaurant, then let his head drop on to the tabletop, mussing up his side parting. 'I just can't wait for all this weirdness to be over, so we can have our nice, normal town back. Well . . . as normal as our town ever is. It's never been particularly "normal" in the normal sense, has it?' Then he shook his head and straightened, grinning. 'OK, how many "normals" was that? Am I over-using it?'

'Well, if you really want people to think that *you're* normal . . .' Olivia teased.

Before she could continue, though, Brendan's face drew into a frown. Peering past her shoulder, out the window, he said, 'Don't look now, but there's this really strange older couple outside. I saw them earlier, and –'

'Let me guess,' Olivia interrupted. 'An elderly gentleman in a tracksuit and a woman wearing a baseball cap? And were they staring suspiciously at everyone who walked past them, like really bad undercover detectives?'

'Yes!' Brendan looked stunned. 'How did you know? Did you notice them earlier?'

'You could say that.' Olivia gave him a rueful smile. 'They're my grandparents.'

'What?' Brendan shook his head. 'The Count and Countess? But Ivy said they're always so elegant and traditional.'

'They're trying to be incognito,' Olivia explained, 'so they can catch the mystery vampire-blogger . . . although to be honest, the Countess doesn't really understand what or who a blogger is.' She lowered her voice to a whisper, but she couldn't hold back a guilty giggle. 'She can't even pronounce the word. She keeps talking about the "blagger"!'

'The *what*?' Brendan laughed too, relaxing in his seat. 'Well, at least that might confuse the blogger if he overhears them.'

'They're not the ones who are in danger from him,' Olivia said grimly. 'At least, not tonight.'

'What are you talking about?' Brendan sat forwards, leaning his elbows on the table. 'All you said in your text was that Ivy was in trouble.'

'She's made an appointment with the blogger,' Olivia whispered. The booths all around them were empty, but she couldn't bear to say the horrible words any louder. 'They're going to meet in the graveyard tonight, at midnight.'

'Are you serious?'

'I wish I wasn't.' Olivia knotted her fingers together. 'It's so dangerous, but she won't see that – you know Ivy, she thinks she can take on anybody! I thought . . . well, maybe . . .'

'I'll go with Ivy,' Brendan said, before she could even ask him. 'Of course I will. I'll keep an eye on her, and on that blogger too. He won't lay a finger on her.'

Olivia's eyes filled with tears. 'Oh, Brendan, thank you so much.' Grabbing a tissue from her bag, she rubbed at her eyes. 'I'm sorry. I don't know what's come over me.' She choked back a sob. 'I just don't know how things got so bad between me and Ivy.'

'Hey.' Brendan reached out a tentative hand, stopping just short of patting her arm. 'Don't worry too much. First Ivy had to go to boarding school, then she hotfooted it back here. It's been crazy!'

'But she *wanted* to be here with us,' Olivia said. 'So why are things so different now?'

Brendan shrugged, but his expression was sympathetic. 'Face it, this time was never going to be easy for either of you. You just have to be patient with each other.'

'I guess so.' Olivia sniffed hard and took a deep breath, wiping away the last of her tears.

'Speak of the devil.' Brendan half-smiled and pointed at the window.

When Olivia turned around, she saw Holly outsite the window, waving madly. Forcing a smile, Olivia shoved her tissue back into her bag and waved back.

'Hey, you!' Holly was standing by their booth a moment later, a whirlwind of energy. 'Why are you wearing a frowny face? Can I buy you a muffin to make you feel better?'

'Oh, I don't really need . . .' Olivia began.

But before she could even finish her sentence, Holly was at the counter pointing towards the biggest, fattest muffin with double cream-cheese icing.

Brendan laughed. 'It looks like you have

someone to look after you for the rest of the afternoon. I'll leave you to it, OK? I'm not really hungry anyway.'

'Aren't you?' Olivia frowned. 'Ivy thinks you're still not eating enough since your illness. Maybe you should –'

'Oh, I'm fine now,' he said carelessly. 'Don't worry about me.' As he slid out of the booth, though, his expression turned serious. He leaned over Olivia, his dark eyes intent. 'Don't worry about Ivy, either,' he whispered. 'I'll keep an eye on her tonight. I promise.'

'Your muffin!' Holly announced a moment later. 'Absolutely designed to make anyone feel better.' As she slid into the booth across from Olivia, she looked around curiously. 'What happened to Broody Boy?'

'You mean Brendan?' Olivia felt a snap of irritation at the nickname, but she told herself not to mind. After all, Brendan was Ivy's boyfriend, and Holly had every reason not to be thrilled with Ivy right now. 'He's off to meet Ivy,' she said, and then moved on quickly before any awkwardness could spring up between them. If there was one person she did not want to discuss with Holly right now, it was her twin. 'How has your day been?'

'Oh, I haven't done much.' Holly shrugged. 'I did take a wander to the mall after I got your text, though, and I saw the book-signing queue. It was quite long, which was good – I want those books to be popular.'

'Of course.' Olivia smiled warmly as she picked up her muffin. *Thank goodness.* Holly was voluntarily telling the truth about going to the mall. *Maybe she had her reasons for lying in the first place.* Anyway, it certainly wasn't the worst lie anyone had ever told.

But why hadn't Holly mentioned speaking with the writer? In fact, S. K. Reardon had told her off quite sternly, but Holly didn't look at all upset about it now.

Something isn't right about this. Olivia set her muffin down without taking a bite, as discomfort twisted through her. She started to open her mouth to ask more – but then she looked at her friend's cheerful expression and the words dried up in her mouth. *Not now.*

She'd seen how Holly tended to react when under stress. Holly had a serious habit of freaking out when she thought she'd upset people. And Olivia couldn't bear to have Holly angry at her too. She needed friends so badly, at the moment. Because Ivy . . .

Olivia swallowed hard, remembering how Ivy had stalked away from her at the mall. She'd never seen her twin so angry at her before.

Who knew what Ivy would do next, in her current mood? For all Olivia knew, Ivy might even decide she wanted to go back to

Wallachia Academy. Why would she want to stay in Franklin Grove when she was so upset at her twin?

Even if Ivy didn't leave again, there was one truth about vampires that neither twin could change. *We might have been born on the same day, but Ivy will live much longer than me*, Olivia thought, with a lump in her throat. *We'll grow apart, no matter how hard we try not to.*

'Well?' Holly said. Gesturing at the cakes on the table between them, she grinned. 'What are you waiting for? We need to eat them before the icing melts!'

'Of course,' Olivia said, and stretched her lips into a smile. 'Let's not waste time!'

Chapter Eight

Despite the neon-bright colours that Ivy's grandparents wore, the atmosphere at the Vega household that night at dinner was as sombre as a tomb. *It's like someone put a stake through our collective hearts*, Ivy thought.

'I cannot believe we still have no clues to this blagger's identity!' the Countess exclaimed. Her steak sat on her plate, uneaten. Out of habit, she reached up to her ear with shaking fingers as if to play with her dangling earrings, but they weren't a part of her undercover outfit. 'After all our detective work and disguises . . .'

'I'm sure you'll find something soon,' Lillian

said soothingly. 'Surely they can't stay anonymous for much longer, not in this day and age.'

'That's what the Queen said.' The Countess looked even more miserable.

Her husband shuddered. 'We phoned Her Majesty before dinner. She was not best pleased by our failure so far.' He took a quick, automatic look at his wrist, where his gold watch usually sat. His wrist was bare. Ivy saw his shoulders slump. 'We'll simply have to work even harder tomorrow.'

Ivy felt her grandparents' unhappiness like a thick cloud of gloom hovering over the table. Even Charles had been subdued. *He hasn't said a word about the wedding all evening!* If Ivy hadn't caught him sneaking peeks at a floral catalogue under the table, when the Count and Countess weren't looking, she would have been seriously worried about him too.

She slid a glance at her twin's unhappy face.

Olivia was barely even pretending to eat her meat-free pasta. Her body was rigid with tension, all because of Ivy's plan.

After the most recent blog entry, just an hour earlier, the entire vampire community had gone into full-on panic.

'*Tonight*,' the blogger had written, '*a major development in our investigation will take place. Some of the vampires' most important secrets will be revealed very soon!*'

It had only taken five minutes from that blog posting for Ivy's grandparents to impose a curfew on every Franklin Grove vampire. They'd stood over Ivy at her computer as she sent the batsqueak alerting the entire community that none of them was to leave their home tonight. Even the Blood Mart was shutting up shop for the first time in its history.

When Olivia looked up from her plate, Ivy had to look away. She couldn't make eye contact with her twin, not now. If their grandparents found out what she was planning to do tonight . . .

'Well,' said Charles, as Horatio appeared to clear away their plates. Sliding out the floral catalogue from underneath the table, he looked around hopefully. 'Perhaps we could take just a few minutes to discuss . . .?'

Lillian put a hand on his arm to cut him off, looking at his parents' weary faces. 'I think maybe it would be best for us all to have an early night.'

'Oh, yes,' said the Countess. She sighed heavily, looking older than Ivy had ever seen her before. 'This day cannot be over soon enough.'

It hasn't even begun, Ivy thought. But she only nodded and forced a yawn, even as anticipation buzzed through her skin. 'I think I'll go to bed now too.'

'Good night,' Olivia said. She kissed both

grandparents on the cheek. 'I'd better go home now.'

'Wait,' Ivy said. 'I'll see you to the door.'

As they walked together down the hallway, Ivy struggled to find anything to say. Talking to her twin had always been easy, but now there was too much tension simmering between them.

How had things become so complicated?

Ivy opened the front door. The sky was already darkening, the air turning chilly as night drew in. She took a deep breath. There were too many words bursting inside her, starting with, *How could you like Holly more than me?* – but she knew she couldn't let herself say any of them.

They stood together in awkward silence for a moment. Finally, Ivy gave up and simply said, 'Be careful on your way home.'

Olivia gave her a sad smile. 'With the curfew you guys just set up, what am I supposed to be afraid of? Vampires?' She started to walk away

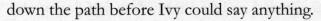

down the path before Ivy could say anything.

We'll fix this, Ivy told herself, as she watched her twin's figure disappear into the darkness. *As soon as I've taken care of the blogger, everything will go back to normal.*

Right now, though, she had to focus on her plan. Her grandparents were already gone by the time she returned to the living room, and Charles was too absorbed in showing Lillian the floral catalogue to give Ivy more than an absent-minded wave goodnight. *Perfect.* Ivy hurried up to her room and climbed into two layers of leggings and a thick leather jacket. It might be summer, but Franklin Grove nights were still cold.

She counted down the hours in her bedroom, listening as the house turned still. Finally, Lillian left for the night, and even Charles and Horatio were tucked up safe and snug in their coffins. Ivy could hear the clock on her wall clicking steadily through the night until . . .

Showtime. She lifted the lid on her coffin and climbed out. Then she slid open her bedroom window and scrambled swiftly down the wisteria plant that grew up the side of the house. She'd had plenty of practice leaping down from it without any problem, but . . . Ivy froze just as she was about to let go of the wisteria and drop down. A horrible, wet, mouldy smell infused her senses, coming from just below her.

Uh-oh. What's that?

She peered down, and her jaw dropped open. *Oh no!*

Horatio had mentioned doing 'a spot of gardening' that afternoon, to keep himself busy and useful. Unfortunately, he hadn't bothered to mention that he'd left a huge pile of yucky compost directly beneath her bedroom window! With her vampire-strong night vision, Ivy could see the snails and worms that writhed in the pile of muck below her.

'Yuck!' She hung on to the wisteria with all her might, her legs flailing. *No way am I dropping into that!* But how was she supposed to get down now?

Male laughter sounded in the darkness. 'Would milady care for a hand?'

Just as Ivy was about to die of a grade-A heart attack, Brendan stepped out of the shadows.

'Ohhh.' Ivy tipped her face against the cool wooden slats of the house, her heart thudding with relief. 'I have never, ever been so glad to see you!' She looked him up and down. 'Though . . . your outfit? Not so much. What are they? Old-man trousers?'

'I thought you might be happy I'm here.' Brendan was shaking with laughter as he put his hands around her waist and swung her to the ground, several inches away from the compost heap. 'And they're chinos, actually. I guess no one mentioned the special new garden decoration to you?'

'Gaaah.' Ivy shuddered as she looked at what she'd nearly fallen into. 'Seriously, though, Brendan. What *are* you doing here?'

'I'm here to be your backup.' Brendan looped one arm around her shoulder. 'Even professional investigative reporters bring photographers with them, don't they? Olivia told me about your plan, so I'm here to make sure you stay safe.'

'Olivia told you?' Ivy grimaced. 'I can't believe she –'

'Oh, c'mon.' Brendan squeezed her shoulder teasingly. 'Are you actually telling me you didn't want me here to save you from the mean old compost heap?'

'Of course I did.' Relaxing, Ivy gave him a quick hug. 'You're my hero. Thank you so much for coming – and for not trying to talk me out of this.'

'Are you kidding?' Brendan shrugged. 'I know you, Ivy. I'm not about to waste my breath. Plus, I want to expose this blogger just as much as you do.'

'Let's do it.'

🦇   🦇   🦇

Lacing her fingers through his, Ivy led the way to the graveyard, feeling lighter than she had all day. *I have to admit, I'm glad he's here. I should say thank you to Olivia tomorrow*, she told herself. Her twin had been thoughtful enough to give Ivy exactly the help she needed – even though she must have been worried that Ivy would be mad at her for interfering.

And maybe when Ivy thanked Olivia for her help, it would finally sort out all the weird awkwardness between them.

Walking through Franklin Grove felt like exploring a completely different town from the one Ivy had known for so long. There were no dark-clothed vampires nodding at her companionably or heading towards the Blood Mart. Instead, they walked through near-empty streets. The only people Ivy and Brendan passed were occasional groups of bunnies, who obviously had no idea that anything was wrong.

Brendan let out a muffled snort as they passed one group of five bunnies wearing identical T-shirts. Lost in her own thoughts, Ivy hadn't paid any attention to them, but after her boyfriend's reaction, she took a look . . . and had to restrain herself from gasping out loud.

Hunt out the Franklin Grove vampires!

'It's a joke,' Brendan whispered into Ivy's ear as she stiffened with outrage. 'Look, they're all laughing. They think the blog's funny, that's all.'

'Right. Hilarious,' Ivy muttered. 'I can't stop laughing.' Her hands clenched into fists.

If all those happy bunnies had any idea how many vampires were hiding at home – scared – tonight, while they all laughed about that blog . . .

'They're looking this way,' Brendan hissed.

Ivy forced a smile as the group members waved and pointed at their shirts. She even managed to follow Brendan's lead and give a hollow laugh at the slogan. But she was still shaking with frustration and anger when they turned off the street a minute later to walk through the tall, spike-tipped iron gates of Franklin Grove's graveyard.

Tombs and headstones loomed in the darkness, while the night wind sighed around them, whispering through Ivy's hair. An owl hooted in the distance, and there were scuttling noises in the undergrowth. As they moved forwards, a twig snapped under Brendan's feet and Ivy almost jumped out of her skin.

Gritting her teeth, she stomped between the graves. *I'm a vampire, not a bunny — I will not be creeped out by this place!*

Gesturing to Brendan, she pressed herself against the side of an old stone tomb the size

163

of a small hut. It was more than big enough to shield them from the sight of anyone arriving.

'Good idea,' Brendan whispered, as he took his place behind her. 'Let's hope the blogger doesn't take too long to show up.'

'If that stupid blogger keeps me waiting . . .' Ivy began. Then she saw a hooded figure arrive at the other end of the graveyard, and she had to bite back a yelp.

Oops. She grimaced, glad that Brendan couldn't see her face. *I guess this place* has *creeped me out a bit after all.*

Creepy atmosphere or not, Ivy wasn't letting any dumb bunny blogger scare her. Craning her neck to keep the hooded figure in her line of vision, she watched carefully as the blogger walked between the graves. Moving from gravestone to family tomb, the figure's face and body were shrouded in darkness. Ivy realised she was holding her breath. Then the person stepped beneath the glow of a streetlight beyond the graveyard's fence and . . .

Oh no, this is as bad as garlic bread for breakfast. Ivy's stomach did a parachute drop as she recognised the face inside the sweatshirt hood and the appliquéd jeans. *Olivia is going to be so upset; I wish I hadn't been right after all.*

She swallowed hard. All day, she'd been excited at the thought of exposing the blogger, and thrilled to have followed the clues to Holly's secret. Now that Ivy saw the other girl on her own in the graveyard in the dead of night, reality hit with a thud. Olivia was going to be crushed . . . and, despite everything, Ivy felt a sudden stab of pity and concern.

Holly had no idea who she was really meeting tonight. For all she knew, she could have put herself in serious danger by coming here. *She must be really desperate. Why is she doing this?*

And, even more importantly, how was Ivy

going to break this to her sister? What if Olivia didn't even believe her – or thought she was just overreacting, out of a dislike of the new girl? Ivy shared a worried glance with Brendan . . . and realised exactly what she needed.

Proof! Reaching into the pocket of her leather jacket, Ivy whipped out her camera. As she started to raise it, though, she hesitated, torn once again by pity. *Holly must be really unhappy, if she has to go to all this trouble and danger just to be noticed . . .*

But I have to do this. It's what I came for! Ivy took a deep, steadying breath. She owed this to the vampire community, to her grandparents . . . and even to Olivia. *She has to know the truth about her friend.*

Gritting her teeth in determination, Ivy snapped three photos in a row – but the sound of the shutter broke the silence in the cemetery.

Holly swirled around. 'Who's there? Come out and show yourselves!'

Drat. No way did Ivy want to confront Holly now, before she'd even had a chance to talk to Olivia about it. She and Brendan both froze, hoping to stay unnoticed.

Footsteps approached. Ivy took a deep breath.

Brendan tapped her shoulder and pointed at a wide crack in the wall of the tomb, leading into deeper darkness. Swallowing down revulsion, Ivy nodded. Together, they squeezed inside the crack. Something soft and slimy squelched around Ivy's legs, and she shuddered. *It's just a pile of old, dead leaves*, she told herself, but that didn't help much, especially when she imagined what kind of creatures might be crawling or wriggling around in those leaves, just like in the compost heap back home. Cobwebs tangled against her cheeks and shoulders. *At least I'm only ruining a stupid bunny outfit*, Ivy thought.

She held her breath as Holly did a circuit of the tomb. Holly's footsteps paused just centimetres from the crack, and Ivy started to feel light-headed with lack of air. Then the footsteps finally retreated. Ivy let out all her held breath in a whoosh.

'Ewww!' She climbed out as fast as she could, dusting herself off.

Brendan followed her, slapping cobwebs off his clothes and kicking his feet against the stone tomb to dislodge slimy leaves. Despite everything, he was grinning widely when he met Ivy's eyes. 'You did it,' he said, 'and you've got absolute proof! May I escort you home now, Madam Detective?'

Ivy bumped shoulders with him. 'Yeah. Let's go home,' she said.

He reached out to take her hand as they walked through the empty streets of Franklin Grove a few minutes later. 'Why aren't you more excited? You cracked the case. The blogger can be outed and she'll stop this crazy hunt of hers.

The whole vampire community is going to be safe, because of you.'

'Maybe,' Ivy said. She sighed.

'So why do you look so sad?'

Ivy shook her head. She felt heavy with unhappiness, especially when she imagined Olivia's reaction to the news. 'One teenage girl has held the whole vampire community to ransom, Brendan. There's something just not right about that.'

'I guess n– uh-oh.' They both came to a dead halt as they turned the corner of Ivy's street. Every light in Ivy's house was blazing – including the light in her bedroom, which she'd left dark. 'That doesn't look good,' Brendan said.

'It looks very, very not good,' Ivy agreed. She gulped. 'Why don't you drop me off here? You can go home and –'

'No way,' Brendan said. 'I'm not leaving you to face it all alone.'

Ivy squeezed his hand gratefully. Together, they walked up the front steps and let themselves into the house.

'There you are!'

The Count and Countess were sitting in their dressing gowns in the living room, as rigid as statues, while Charles paced back and forth, quivering with tension. He swung around when Ivy stepped into the doorway. She flinched at the expression in his eyes. She'd never seen him look so angry . . . or so scared.

'What on earth do you think you were playing at, young lady?' the Countess demanded. 'Sneaking out with your boyfriend on a night like this?'

'That's not . . .' Ivy began, but her father interrupted her.

'You might be interested to know,' he said coldly, 'that the wind blew your window shut and woke us. Did you really think that no one would notice you slipping out? Tonight of all nights?

170

Did you think we wouldn't care?'

The Count glowered at her. 'Did or did not your grandmother make it clear that no vampire was to leave their home tonight?'

Horatio slipped into the room, carrying a tray of steaming hot chocolate with whipped cream. Ivy turned to him gratefully. 'Oh, thank y–'

'This is no time for hot chocolate!' the Count bellowed. With a wave of his arm, he sent Horatio out of the room, still carrying the tray.

Uh-oh. Ivy exchanged a nervous look with Brendan. *If even Grandpa is turning down sweet treats, then things really are bad.*

'I have never in my life been so disappointed,' the Countess said heavily. 'It was bad enough for you to leave Wallachia Academy without any consideration for our feelings, but to flout our authority so blatantly tonight – at such a time! It is unbelievable. All I can think is that you refuse to consider yourself a part of our community.'

171

She shook her head, her expression weary. 'Ivy, you have seriously let us down . . . *again*.'

Ivy's throat burned as emotion choked her. She opened her mouth to say something, anything . . .

But Brendan was already speaking: 'Wait a minute.' He fixed the Countess with a fearless glance. 'None of you has stopped to ask Ivy what she was really doing tonight. She wasn't turning her back on the community. She was *saving* it.'

The Count glowered at him. 'What are you talking about, young man?'

'Sure, she took a risk, but only because she was so close to finding out the truth,' Brendan said. 'And she got it too. Ivy found out who the blogger is! She set up a stake out and even got photos.'

The Countess gasped. Her hand flew to her throat. Horatio edged back into the room, still holding his tray of chocolate – obviously he must have been listening from outside.

Ivy's father put one hand on her shoulder.

Gently, he asked, 'Ivy? Will you please tell all of us who our arch-enemy is?'

Arch-enemy? Ivy swallowed hard. It wasn't like her dad to use such grand terms. 'Arch-enemy' sounded historical, dramatic . . . dangerous.

She took a deep breath. 'Our arch– I mean, the *blogger* is . . . Holly.'

China rattled as Horatio lost his grip on his tray. He caught it just in time, but none of the gathered vamps said a word. They looked too stunned to speak.

Finally, Charles shook his head. Speaking slowly, as if he were still processing the information, he said, 'Olivia's friend? The person we let into our home? But that's not – she couldn't –'

'Just look.' Ivy showed him the photos on her camera, and her grandparents and Horatio all gathered round to see for themselves.

'There's no denying it, then,' Charles said sadly, as he gazed down at the last photo.

The Countess still looked oddly fragile with shock. 'How are we going to confront this girl?'

'We can't,' Ivy said. She'd been thinking as hard as she could all the way home. No, she didn't like Holly, but she loved Olivia . . . and there was a better way to handle this, one that didn't involve arch-enemies and anger. Of course she wasn't going to let the vampire community stay in fear, but sometimes misdirection was better than attack.

She lifted her chin and looked her grandparents in the eyes. 'I'm not sure we confront her, when we still don't know why she's doing this. But we could find out.'

Her father frowned. 'And how are we supposed to do that?'

'Well,' Ivy said. 'There's someone Holly really, really likes . . . *Olivia*.'

Ivy didn't tell her dad or grandparents the part that really scared her. If they were going to ask Olivia for her help, she would have to make a choice about who mattered most to her – Ivy or Holly. And for the first time since they had met, Ivy couldn't be sure where Olivia's loyalty would lie.

Chapter Nine

Olivia was still asleep when her cell phone rang the next morning. It had taken her hours to finally drop off — she couldn't stop worrying about what Ivy was up to. She woke only just in time to grab the phone and mumble, 'Wha— ?'

'We need you over here right now,' Ivy said. Her voice sounded tense. 'Emergency meeting at my house. Please.'

Olivia bit back all the anxious questions she wanted to ask. Before anything else, she needed to see that her twin was safe after last night's adventure. 'I'm on my way.'

She scrambled into a pink vest and a pair of white Capri pants. Barely five minutes later she was fully dressed and ready to go.

Her adoptive parents both stared at her as she raced downstairs. 'My goodness,' Mrs Abbott said. 'We don't usually see you up so early on a weekend.'

'I got a call from Ivy,' Olivia explained, and forced a smile. 'She's cooking me a special breakfast.'

'That's nice, dear,' Mrs Abbott said.

Mr Abbott beamed at her over his newspaper. 'As Henry David Thoreau once said: "Let us rise early and fast, or break fast, gently and without perturbation."'

'Um,' Olivia said. She remembered the tension in Ivy's voice, and thought of the emergency meeting waiting for her. *I think there might be plenty of perturbation, actually.* 'I'll try,' she told her adoptive dad. 'But I should really hurry now, or the breakfast might burn.'

Both of her parents smiled indulgently and waved her off as she ran out of the house and jumped on to her bicycle. As she cycled to her twin's house at top speed, worries swirled through her head. What could have gone wrong last night to make Ivy sound so worried and upset even now? Had she been exposed as a vampire in front of the blogger? Worse yet, had she been hurt?

By the time she reached the Vega house, Olivia was feeling so frantic she jumped off her bike and left it sprawled on the lawn, in too much of a rush to prop it up neatly. She let herself in the front door and hurried inside to find the household in utter chaos.

She stopped in the dining-room doorway, staring in disbelief. A plate of smoked kippers sat ignored in the centre of the table while the Count and Countess were hunched over a laptop with

Ivy. Olivia would never have believed that the rigidly proper Countess would allow computers at the table during a meal!

Meanwhile, Horatio seemed to be having a nervous breakdown in the kitchen. Olivia could hear Lillian making soothing noises, but his voice rose above hers in a near-wail: 'If this bread doesn't finish baking in the next five minutes the whole meal will be ruined!'

Mr Vega stomped into the room behind Olivia, a clothing catalogue in his hand. 'Quick, everyone: pick out more bunny clothes! The uglier, the better.'

'Don't we have enough already?' Ivy said, without looking away from the screen of the laptop.

'Who knows how long the VITs will be in town? And Horatio has got enough on his plate without having to wash a bunch of bunny clothes.'

Olivia was impressed: her bio-dad finally

seemed to be really getting into the spirit of all this! Until now, he'd always seemed too distracted to completely participate. She gave him an approving smile.

He leaned over to mutter in her ear on his way to the table, 'I was *meant* to be getting ready for this afternoon's engagement party by now!'

Aha. Olivia hid a smile. There was still a little bit of the Groomzilla lurking beneath her bio-dad's surface after all.

'There you are!' Ivy finally turned around and saw Olivia. Looking even paler than usual, she gave a weak smile and waved Olivia over. 'Um, there's something I need to tell you.'

'We'll be back in just a moment, my dears.' The Countess rose hastily, giving her husband a meaningful look. 'I think Horatio may need some calming in the kitchen.'

'He is a perfectionist, you know!' the Count said jovially. 'That's why his bread is so excellent.'

Despite his hearty tone, Olivia caught the worry in his eyes as he looked from one granddaughter to the other.

Uh-oh.

Olivia waited until their grandparents had left the room before she moved cautiously to perch on the chair next to Ivy's. *What's this about?* Olivia thought. *I can't bear another argument.* The air felt thick with tension. Olivia clasped her hands together to keep them from tapping on the table. 'What's wrong?'

'First . . .' Ivy took a deep breath. 'I want to apologise to you for being so tetchy lately.'

Olivia felt a rush of relief. 'That's OK.' She shrugged, but it was an effort to smile. *Don't cry! Whatever you do, don't cry!* 'I understand it's been a tricky time.'

'I'm still sorry.' Ivy reached into a bag that sat underneath the table. 'And I made this for you.'

Olivia gasped. A pretty pink corsage lay in

her sister's pale hand. Mingled in with the pink blossoms, she saw pink rhinestones.

Now tears really burned behind Olivia's eyes. She knew exactly why Ivy had picked those rhinestones – to match the pink rhinestone cowboy hat Jackson had once bought Olivia, the one she still cherished even after everything that had happened.

Nobody knew her as well as her sister.

Olivia's smile was wobbly as she blinked back her tears. 'Didn't you come out in hives, just making the thing? I thought you were allergic to pink.'

'I'm not allergic to anything about you.' Ivy reached over and pinned the corsage to Olivia's T-shirt, her long dark hair falling around her face. 'Will you forgive me for being such an idiot?'

Olivia threw her arms around Ivy, finally letting the tears escape. 'Of course I will. You're my best friend, and you *always* will be.'

As she spoke the words, all the tension she'd been carrying for days fell away from her, and she realized it was the truth. This summer might have been strained, but she knew without a doubt that one thing would always be true: her twin would always be there for her.

'Well.' Ivy's eyes looked suspiciously red as she drew back; she sniffed hard. 'Talking of friends . . .' She stiffened her shoulders, looking as if she were bracing herself for an attack. 'You need to see this.'

She turned the laptop round so that Olivia could see what was on the screen.

Olivia leaned forwards, peering at the group of thumbnail-sized photos. 'Headstones. It's the graveyard.'

'That's right. Where I went to meet the vampire hunter.' Ivy took a deep breath and clicked on the last thumbnail. 'And there she is: Holly. She's the blogger.'

'What?!' Olivia threw herself back in the chair. Her heartbeat sped up until it hurt her chest. 'I can't believe it.'

Ivy looked miserable. 'I promise I wouldn't make it up.'

'I know that,' Olivia shook her head. 'I mean, the evidence is right in front of me. But Holly . . .!' She stared at the photo: Holly's face shadowed by the hood of her sweatshirt as she stood between two headstones.

Holly was the blogger, the one who'd threatened Olivia's family and their friends. Holly, who'd been so kind to Olivia, such a good friend to her. Holly . . .

Olivia swallowed hard and tried to think logically, even though the betrayal made her burn. 'The thing is, despite what you think of her, I just can't believe that she's really a bad person. She must have a reason for doing this.'

'Olivia . . .'

'Ever since I met her, my instinct has always been to trust her.'

'I understand that.' From the strain on Ivy's face, Olivia could see that her twin was working hard to stay outwardly calm and reasonable. 'But can you see that some of the things Holly's been saying just don't match up?'

Olivia bit her lip. She didn't answer.

'For example . . .' Ivy leaned forwards. 'Remember how she said she might be too shy to meet that author? But from the way she spoke to him at the book-signing – and the way he recognised her at first sight – it definitely looked as if that wasn't their first chat.'

'She was really upset at the end of it,' Olivia said slowly. 'And the author seemed so angry about something she'd done.'

Ivy frowned. 'You know, you're right. He didn't just seem annoyed, the way he would be at a fan who was getting pushy. He looked almost *disappointed* angry.' She paused, her frown deepening. 'There was something about his expression that looked familiar to me at the time, but I couldn't figure out what it was.'

'What do you mean?' Olivia asked. 'Had you met him somewhere before?'

'No,' Ivy said. 'But I've seen that expression a lot lately – on my *angry relatives*.'

Olivia sucked in a breath as the realisation rocketed through her. 'Could that be it? She's always talking about *Bare Throats at Sunset*. But if she was somehow related to the author, why wouldn't she have said so? And what's this got to do with the blog?'

'There's only one way to find out,' Ivy said.

'You're right.' Olivia sighed. 'It's time to talk to Holly and find out the truth.'

She stood up, steeling herself. When she turned around, though, she saw the Countess standing in the doorway. The Count and their dad came to stand behind her.

'There's absolutely no reason for you girls to bother yourselves any more,' their grandmother said warmly. 'You've done a brilliant job investigating, but now we'll deal with Holly.'

Olivia felt a ripple of uneasiness. 'What do you mean "deal with Holly"?'

'Oh, nothing to worry about.' The Countess waved a hand through the air. 'A mere case of . . . misdirecting her. We've been doing it for centuries. How else do you think we could have kept ourselves secret for so long?'

Behind her, the Count nodded sternly. Even Olivia's bio-dad had a hard, business-like look on his face. She felt a flutter of nerves as she looked around the circle of faces.

No matter what her mistakes had been, Holly was Olivia's friend. And now Olivia's grandmother was talking about their way to 'deal with' their current problem?

'The look on your face!' The Countess began to laugh, raising one hand to her mouth. 'Oh, Olivia, my dear, no, no, *no*! There's not a thing for you to worry about, I promise.'

But still . . .

Ivy stepped up to Olivia's side. 'Can you just put things on hold for a few hours? The two of us might be able to handle this quietly.'

The Countess frowned. 'My dears, this is a serious matter.'

'We know that,' Olivia said. 'But we have a strategy we want to try out first. Isn't that right, Ivy?'

She kept her gaze fixed on her grandmother's face, but in the corner of her eye, she saw Ivy looking at her bug-eyed. She wasn't surprised – she hadn't had a chance to share the plan she was forming. But surely . . .

Yes. Like the faithful twin she was, Ivy nodded in agreement, on Olivia's side as always. 'We

188

do,' Ivy confirmed. 'Will you trust us enough to try it? Please?'

The Countess's eyes flickered over to Ivy. Her face turned grim. 'Can you promise me that you won't let us down this time?'

Olivia winced. She knew her hot-tempered twin. How much needling could Ivy take before she finally lost her patience? If that happened, everything could be lost.

But when she turned to look at Ivy, she found her twin the picture of calm composure. Ivy looked straight into their grandmother's eyes as she spoke, her voice clear and confident: 'Grandma, I have never let you down before.'

'Oh?' The Countess arched one eyebrow, her face hardening. 'Have you already forgotten Wallachia Academy? Did our wishes mean so little to you then?'

'Never,' Ivy repeated. 'You and Grandpa will always be important to me – but I've always

189

made the choices that were true to myself. Isn't that what the best vampires do?'

For a moment, Olivia couldn't breathe as she watched emotions flicker across their grandmother's face – irritation, surprise and then finally acceptance.

The Countess nodded as graciously as a queen. 'I understand,' she said. Her face softened, and she reached out to lay one hand on Ivy's shoulder. 'Yes, girls. I trust you both. Do what you have to.'

'Thank you!' Olivia gasped. She traded a relieved glance with Ivy and hurried out of the kitchen.

'Go on, then,' the Countess called after them. 'But if you can't resolve this issue by dusk, we'll have to do it *our* way.'

'We understand,' Ivy said.

Olivia pulled Ivy to a halt at the living-room door. Inside, her dad was glumly ordering ugly

clothes online while wedding catalogues lay
ignored at his feet.

'Dad?' Olivia said. 'Can we invite a friend to
your engagement party?'

'Of course!' His expression lightened for the
first time that morning as he looked up at Olivia.
'It's nice to have someone remember what's
really important around here.' With a guilty look
towards the dining room, he nudged one of his
wedding catalogues open with the toe of his shoe
and took a quick peek inside.

'What are you doing?' Ivy whispered. 'Why do
you want to invite someone? You can't –'

'Don't worry,' Olivia whispered back, pulling
her twin out through the front door. 'I have a
really good idea.'

🦇   🦇   🦇

The trip to Holly's house was just long enough
for Ivy to hear Olivia's whole plan. Ivy was still
feeling nervous about it as they walked up the

front steps, but all it took was a glance at the pink corsage on Olivia's shirt to remind her what was really important.

Her twin had chosen to trust her. Ivy couldn't do any less for Olivia now.

She pushed the doorbell and fixed a smile on her face. *No more grumpy Ivy*, she promised herself.

'Hey.' Holly opened the door, looking from one twin to another. 'What are you guys doing here? It's kind of early for a visit.'

Olivia beamed, reminding Ivy what a good actress her sister really was. If the Hollywood industry strikes ever ended, her twin would become a true star. 'Can we come in to talk for just a minute?'

'Of course.' Holly stepped aside to let them in. As usual, she was wearing her trademark hippy clothes: a tie-dyed T-shirt and jeans with flowers and suns embroidered all over them. *Not exactly what I'd expect from a vampire hunter*, Ivy thought.

Then she stepped inside, and her eyes widened. The bookshelves in Holly's front room were lined with rows and rows of *Bare Throats at Sunset*. 'Wow,' she said. 'You must *really* like that book!'

'Yeah, well . . .' Holly's face coloured. Her long blonde hair fell over her eyes as she looked down at her feet. 'You said you wanted to talk?'

'We wanted to invite you to a party at our house this afternoon, at three o'clock,' Olivia said brightly.

'A *special* kind of party,' Ivy added meaningfully.

'Sorry?' Holly frowned.

'Lots of people are going to be there,' Olivia said. 'Lots of *different* kinds of people.'

'That's right.' Ivy lowered her voice to a whisper. 'It's, um, *super-secret*. With a *very exclusive guest list*. That's why we're having to use a *special menu.*'

Come on! She urged Holly mentally. *Get the picture!*

Between her tone of voice and the thing she was doing with her eyebrows, it had to be obvious what she meant: *Vampires!*

Holly's lips twitched. 'Well,' she said. 'That does sound . . . *interesting.*'

Had they done it? Ivy felt her muscles tense up as she waited for Holly to continue. *Please let the plan work!* It all depended on what Holly did next. Had she figured out that the twins knew she was behind the blog? Or would she remain under her deep cover of a normal girl of Franklin Grove?

Not that anyone in this town is normal anyway, Ivy thought ruefully. Still, she held her breath as she waited for Holly to make up her mind.

Finally, Holly nodded, and Ivy let out her breath in a whoosh.

'OK,' Holly said. 'I'd love to come!'

'See you this afternoon!' Ivy said. *Job well done.*

As soon as she and Olivia were safely out of sight of Holly's home, they gave each other a high five – then they both started to run for the Vegas' house.

They had a lot of work to do in the next few hours.

Chapter Ten

Ivy had never seen her dad look quite so happy. When she'd announced that the whole family would pitch in to get the house ready for the engagement party, she could have sworn she saw tears of joy in his eyes. Less than a minute later, he was in full Groomzilla mode, snapping orders and striding around the house with a bounce to his step and a determined gleam in his eye.

It was just what the twins needed.

By that afternoon, an enormous balloon arch surrounded the front door, bursting with colourful balloons that Olivia and the Count had inflated while the Countess had worked on the flower arrangements. Horatio had been cooking for hours, and the scent of delicious food filled the house.

Even Ivy had spent time in the kitchen, making special burgers to try to tempt Brendan into recovering his appetite. Remembering the last time she'd tried that, at the ill-fated baking party, she winced – then added more meat to the burgers.

At least there won't be any garlic in these ones!

As Mr Vega mixed some very special cocktails, the doorbell rang. Ivy took off her apron, gave her hands a quick wash, and smoothed down her boring sweatpants. *Let's hope I never have to wear these again after today!*

Olivia was waiting for her in the hallway, her eyes bright with nervous anticipation. Together, the twins opened the door.

'Hey,' Brendan said.

Thank goodness, he was looking more like his normal self again, not so dangerously thin as he'd looked even a few days before. Ivy's shoulders slumped in relief. Before she could say a word, though, he hurried into the house, looking nervously over his shoulder. He slammed the door behind himself as quickly as if he were trying to escape pursuit.

'What's going on out there?' he said. 'Did you know there's a whole crowd of people outside your house? I had to shove my way through just to get here.'

'Really?' Ivy darted to the window, closely followed by Olivia. At the end of the driveway people were milling around, trying to look as casual as if they just happened to be hanging out . . . but there was no way that such a massive crowd would ever have gathered on the Vegas' quiet street on a normal afternoon.

'Wait,' Olivia said. 'I recognise that man – I saw

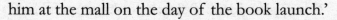

him at the mall on the day of the book launch.'

Ivy followed her sister's gaze to a blond man in a long trench coat. She shuddered. 'I remember him. He was wearing a garlic necklace.' She pointed. 'And there's that girl who was taking photos at the mall. Look – she's taking a photo of the house down the street right now!' Ivy gave Olivia a mischievous grin. 'Should I lean out and wave to let her know she's got the wrong address?'

'No!' Olivia yanked Ivy back and twitched the curtains shut. She couldn't hide her grin, but her tone was stern. 'You know the plan.'

'I know,' Ivy said, grinning back at her. 'Let's go find out how all those people knew to come here.'

Together with Brendan, the twins settled in front of Ivy's computer. Ivy opened the vampire-hunting blog and frowned. 'No update,' she said. 'So how did they find out?'

'Try BirdChirp,' Olivia said.

'I beg your pardon?' Ivy let out a scornful huff of air.

Brendan said, 'Um, Olivia . . . do you have any idea how much more advanced batsqueaks are? They're so much faster than the human version.'

Olivia rolled her eyes. 'I'm talking about checking the blogger's BirdChirp account, you guys, not switching to BirdChirp yourselves. Come on. It may not be as cool as the batsqueaks you guys use, but it's as close as humans come. Plus, there's a link from the blog to a BirdChirp account. See? It's worth a try.'

'OK, if you really want . . .' Shrugging, Ivy clicked the link from the vampire-hunting blog to its BirdChirp account (*FrnklinGrvVamps*). Then she stiffened. 'A-ha!'

'*What blood-sucking excitement might be happening on Undertaker Hill at 3 p.m. today? Just wait and see . . .*'

The chirp had been posted six hours ago – just after they'd left Holly's house.

Another chirp followed it, posted just an hour ago.

'*Have you set your stopwatches, vampire hunters? Only one hour to go . . .*'

'Well, it looks like Holly's taken the bait,' Ivy said.

'Yeah, I guess so,' Olivia said. Ivy hated to see how downcast her sister looked. Misery shone in Olivia's eyes, but her expression was resigned. 'Don't worry, Ivy. I'm not arguing any more. The evidence is pretty damning.'

Ivy wanted to reach out and hug her. *It's finally hit home. The girl she trusted is behind all this.*

The doorbell rang again.

'Well.' Olivia stood up, smoothing down the glittering pink minidress she'd put on for the party. She smiled as brightly as the Hollywood star that she should have been by now, if only her first big film role hadn't been delayed. 'We'd better get started.'

As they left Ivy's bedroom, they heard Mr Vega open the front door. 'Holly! It's so nice to see you here again.' He led her into the living room, where the Count and Countess were waiting, wearing their most garish pink-and-orange checked outfits and their stiffest expressions. 'May I introduce you to my parents? Mom, Dad, this is Holly, one of Olivia's best friends. Isn't it nice to have her here with us today?'

The Count shook Holly's hand, his expression tight. The Countess nodded. Her smile looked as if it had been glued on to her face by force – and was about to slip right off.

'Um . . . hi,' Holly said. As she turned to Ivy, Olivia and Brendan, she looked sheepish.

The adults moved discreetly to a different part of the room – which, Ivy knew, wouldn't stop them from listening to everything with their vampire super-hearing. But it was time for Ivy and Olivia to take over.

'Holly!' Ivy smiled broadly. 'Hey, did you have to squeeze past that crowd in the street?'

Holly grimaced, looking guilty. 'Uh, yeah, I did. What's up with that?'

'I wondered about that too,' Brendan said. 'They look like they're waiting for something.'

Ivy raised her eyebrows. 'Anyone would think that *someone* has been spreading rumours about something special happening.'

Holly opened her mouth to speak.

Before she could utter a word, Olivia said softly, 'I can't imagine who would do such a thing.'

Two red spots appeared on Holly's cheeks. 'I'm so sorry,' she said, all in a rush. 'I'm the reason all those people are there. I may have mentioned on my blog that there was a gathering, a good place to spot vampires.'

Olivia was shaking her head. 'Why would you do that?'

'There's a good reason . . .' Holly started to say, but Ivy cut her off.

'I found something interesting.' She reached into the boring sports bag that was part of her bunny disguise, and pulled out a copy of *Bare Throats at Sunset*.

Holly's brow creased in confusion. 'I thought you hated that book.'

'I read it again more carefully,' Ivy said. 'And guess what I noticed, this time around?' She flipped to page 56. 'Listen to the description of the main character's daughter: "She had hippy jeans, long strawberry-blonde hair and a pale face" . . . interesting, huh? It sounds just like someone I know.'

Holly's face turned beetroot red. 'I'm sorry! It's true. I should have told you guys.' She wrapped her arms around her chest, seeming to shrink under their combined gaze. 'My dad wrote the book.'

'But your last name isn't Reardon,' Olivia said. No longer acting, all her hurt was in her face. 'Or were you lying about that too?'

'His name isn't really S. K. Reardon,' Holly said. 'It's Sean Turner. Reardon is my grandma's maiden name.'

'But if he's your dad,' said Ivy, 'why didn't you say so before? Why did you pretend you didn't know him?'

Holly swallowed visibly, looking as if she were fighting back tears. 'I almost never get to see him any more. He lives in San Francisco. Every time I've seen him recently, he's just been so upset that his book is selling badly. It was his big dream to get it published, but no one cared. No one was buying it. And it's so unfair! It's not nearly as bad as some other vampire books that are *really* popular – no matter what you think of it!'

Ivy winced. 'I'm really sorry I said that the writing was terrible,' she said. 'I wouldn't have done that if I knew he was your dad. And . . .' She struggled with her pride, and finally managed to admit the truth. 'It isn't really all that bad,' she said. 'I was just upset that you dissed *Shadowtown*.'

Holly's lips twitched. 'You can't pretend *that*'s a classic, either.'

'No,' Ivy agreed. 'But I love it anyway. Shows how much taste I've got, huh?'

For the first time ever, she and Holly shared a real smile.

Holly's smile faded quickly, though. 'I just wanted to do something to help my dad.' She bit her lip and glanced at the windows of the house and the crowd outside. 'That's why I set up the blog. Have you figured it all out?'

Olivia sighed, leaning into Ivy. 'Why don't you tell us in your own words?'

Ivy put one hand on her sister's arm in support. It had to hurt Olivia to hear this from her friend.

Holly spoke quickly. 'I just thought if I could make people think there were *actual* vampires living in a small American town, I could really have an effect. I could create an Internet sensation, you know? I'd fuel interest in vampires and sell more copies of my dad's book to coincide with his book-signing here. There are a lot of vampire books out right now – it's so hard for a new one to get noticed! But if there were rumours about *real* vampires existing, and people thought S. K. Reardon might have "insider info" –'

'Then his book would have an edge,' Ivy finished for her.

'I just wanted to help him, that's all.' Holly's shoulders slumped. 'But he didn't see it that way.' She looked down at the floor as she added softly, 'I haven't spoken to him since he told me off at the mall. Believe me, this plan could not have backfired any more spectacularly.'

Despite everything, Ivy couldn't help her heart

beginning to melt. *I can't believe this is happening to me!* But the misery in Holly's voice was heart-breaking.

'Come on,' Ivy said. 'Let's go out to the garden to get a bit of privacy.'

The Count and Countess would know everything they needed to by now. It felt wrong to let Holly unburden herself any more when she didn't know how many people were listening to her story.

Holly didn't resist as Ivy and Olivia led her outside. Brendan shut the door firmly behind them and stood guard inside the house.

'I'm sorry,' Holly said, as she sagged down on to one of the garden chairs. 'I messed everything up, and not just with my dad. It felt like a fun game, pretending that vampires might be real . . . but I should never have used you guys as part of it.'

'No,' Olivia said. 'You shouldn't have.

But . . .' She traded a glance with Ivy.

Ivy nodded, letting go of the last of her resentment. She might be grumpy, but she couldn't deny the truth. 'We can all understand that family comes first.'

'My dad doesn't understand it.' Tears streaked Holly's face. 'I really thought he would be happy, even proud of me for doing it, but it was just a disaster.'

'Not completely,' Ivy said. 'I mean, your plan did kind of work. Look at how all those people were queuing up at the mall to get their books signed!'

'It's true,' Olivia said, putting an encouraging hand on Holly's arm. 'I'm sure he'll realize soon that you were only trying to help, even if you did go about it the wrong way.'

'But . . .'

Holly stopped, frowning, as they were all distracted by a sudden commotion inside the house. They heard raised voices. A moment later, the door burst open. An unexpected figure strode into the garden, waving an all-too-familiar book.

'Woot! I've got it, and it's mine, all mine!'

Ivy's mouth dropped open. 'Mr Harker?'

She rubbed her eyes. Beside her, she saw Olivia looking as if she'd seen a ghost.

Jacob Harker, the hot-shot movie producer who'd offered Olivia her first starring role, had just burst into their garden, waving *Bare Throats at Sunset* over his head.

Chapter Eleven

*H*arker! Has he come all the way from California? Olivia shook her head. He'd become friends with the girls after Olivia acted in one of his films, but she'd never expected to see him in Franklin Grove again. 'What are you doing here?'

He waved his copy of *Bare Throats at Sunset* like a flag. 'I'm here to celebrate with your dad and Lillian, of course! But I'm killing two birds with one stone – I've just discovered this book and it's *gold*, dudes. I'm buying the film rights.'

All three girls looked at him, absolutely stunned.

'*What?*' Holly croaked.

Lillian stepped into the garden behind him, smiling. 'I sent him a copy of the novel to read, and he loved it just as much as I did.'

'But – but . . .' Holly stuttered. 'You don't mean . . .'

Olivia leaned over and touched Holly's arm. 'Mr Harker is big in the film business. This could be the best thing ever for your dad.'

'No time to chat!' Harker said, interrupting. He obviously hadn't heard Olivia, or made the connection between Holly and the author of the book he was holding. He swept his arms out expansively. 'I've got to find him! The dude of the hour! Reardon's supposed to be in Franklin Grove for the book tour, right? I've got to talk to him about this book – it's going to be *huge* once it's on the big screen, and I want his input along the way. We're talking mega-blockbuster-spectacular, guys!'

'*Mega* . . .' Holly whispered. Her eyes looked

glazed with shock.

'There's just one problem. I can't find him!' He rolled his eyes. 'Does the dude not realise he's a hot commodity? The strikes are finally over, and I need him *now*!'

Olivia saw her sister smirk. 'I know exactly who can help you,' Ivy said, glancing at Holly.

'Holly?' Olivia said. She smiled gently. 'I bet your dad would like to hear from you now.' *My heart could just melt right now*, she thought. This was like the best Hollywood drama ever!

'I don't know if he'll even answer the phone,' Holly whispered. She sniffed, wiping the tears hastily off her cheeks. 'But of course I'll try.' She took a deep breath and pulled out her cell phone. Olivia watched the colour in her cheeks fluctuate as she waited for her dad's answer. Then she said, 'Dad? It's me, but . . . there's a Hollywood producer here who wants to talk to you. No, I didn't – it's not –'

'Here, give me that!' Harker scooped the phone out of her hands. 'Harker of Harker Films here, Reardon. Get your butt over here, man! I want to shake hands on our film deal!'

Olivia smiled. Ivy was grinning widely, her arms folded as she watched Harker shout into the phone.

'I'm so glad I'm back in Franklin Grove to see all this,' she said. 'It was totally worth that stake out in the graveyard!'

Olivia shook her head. 'Just promise me you'll never take a risk like that again. I'm so glad Brendan was around to look after you last night.'

Ivy rolled her eyes. 'Do you seriously think I need looking after?'

Olivia flung an arm around her sister's shoulders and pulled her in for a hug. 'Not even by me?' she asked. *I'll never stop looking out for my vampire twin*, she added to herself.

Ivy shrugged her off, but gently. 'OK, OK, you can stick with me if you like,' she said. Olivia knew she was secretly enjoying the moment, even if it would have killed Ivy to admit it.

'I'm not going anywhere,' Olivia told her.

Ivy grinned and linked arms with her. 'That's two of us, then.'

🦇   🦇   🦇

When Holly's dad arrived at the house fifteen minutes later, Ivy ran for the door, but Charles got there first.

The house was full of family and friends from Franklin Grove, Transylvania, and California, all talking and laughing and eating the gourmet food her dad had chosen so carefully. After all the distractions of the past few days, Mr Vega's long-awaited engagement party was not only happening, it was chock-full of celebrities, and he was glowing with pride.

'Mr Turner!' Charles gushed as he opened the

door. 'I'm so thrilled. A real live author here for such a special occasion! Lillian and I are both so honoured.'

'We are pleased to meet you, Mr Turner,' Lillian said calmly. Standing beside her fiancé, she looked as composed and elegant as ever in a sleek burgundy dress, completely unfazed by their unexpected guest. 'Your daughter is in the garden, waiting for you.'

'Oh, thank goodness. The last time we saw each other, I – well, I really need to talk to her, to apologise. I shouldn't have been so stern with her. Sorry, you don't need to hear all that, do you?' Looking pale and shocked, the author reached up to straighten his tie with a trembling hand. When his gaze landed on the Count and Countess standing in the corner of the room, drinking cocktails and chatting with Lillian's parents, he gave a nervous twitch.

The Count beamed at him and waved. They

were separated by the crowd, but even a human could read the Count's lips as he mouthed happily: *'I've still got that pizza recipe for you! I'll give it to you later.'*

Mr Turner blinked, shook his head, and turned back to his host. 'I'm sorry, Mr Vega, but could I just check – is there really a Hollywood producer here too? And he really wants to see me? My daughter said on the phone –'

'Oh, yes, yes.' Looking smug, Charles led Holly's dad through the crowded house, towards the garden, where Harker and Holly both waited. 'He's a friend of my fiancée, you know. She loved your book, so – oh!' He suddenly came to a halt, looking inspired. 'You don't take commissions, do you?'

'Commissions?' Mr Turner blinked. 'I'm not sure I understand . . .'

'Novelisations of real-life weddings, for example?'

Oh no. Behind them, Ivy rolled her eyes. She heard Olivia choke. Groomzilla had struck again!

Luckily, Lillian had been close enough to overhear. 'Come along, darling. I think Mr Turner has plenty to think about already. Mr Turner, may I introduce Jacob Harker? Jacob, Mr Turner will be with you in just a moment, but I think he needs a minute alone with his daughter first.' Putting one hand on her fiancé's arm, she gently dragged Charles back inside and closed the glass door to the garden.

As they left, Ivy could hear her father saying, 'But wouldn't it be a brilliant idea, sweetheart? We could hand copies out to all the guests – we could even start a wedding blog to promote it!'

'Oh no!' Ivy's jaw dropped open.

Behind her, she heard her twin's giggle. Ivy turned to meet Olivia's eyes. 'She will stop him, won't she?' Ivy said.

'I think Franklin Grove has had enough

218

blogging to last a century,' Olivia agreed. 'And can you imagine Grandma's face if she found out there was a would-be *blagger* in the family?'

Ivy snorted with laughter. 'She'd have a fit.' She shook her head. 'You're right. I don't think we have to worry about groomzilla-dot-com popping up any time soon, no matter what Dad might think.'

Together, they looked out into the garden, where Holly and her dad were sharing an enormous hug. Mr Harker stood nearby, tapping his foot impatiently, but it looked like Hollywood was going to have to wait – 'S. K. Reardon' was putting his daughter first. When Holly finally stepped back, her dad draped one arm around her shoulder before he turned to the waiting producer.

'Do you want me to tell you what they're saying?' Ivy asked Olivia. She knew the glass door was too thick for her twin to overhear without super-strong vamp hearing.

Olivia shook her head, though, smiling as she watched Harker's first words put a look of amazed joy on the author's face. 'There's no need,' she said. 'I can tell exactly what's going on out there.'

Within a minute, Turner and Harker were talking excitedly, while Holly beamed at them both, shining with happiness.

'And now there's no more need for Holly's blog either,' Ivy said. 'Whew.'

'Thank goodness,' Olivia said. 'Let's give them some privacy.'

They moved into the living room, sharing a secret smile. As they stood by the window, just far enough from the other party guests, Olivia murmured, 'I can't believe we wriggled out of this mess – and without anyone getting hurt on the way.'

'You're telling me.' Ivy sighed. 'I know we

won't always be so lucky . . . but I'm glad we were this time.' Linking arms with Olivia, she rested her head on her twin's shoulder. *I must be going soft in my old age*, she thought.

Outside the window, the crowd of VITs was still milling around, but Ivy didn't care about any of them any more. While they'd waited for Holly's dad to arrive, Holly had promised to close down the blog – and to write a final post explaining that it had all been just a hoax. It was a blog post that would take real courage to write. *But I'm finally beginning to see that Holly had courage and loyalty all along.* Even Ivy Vega could admit when she'd been wrong – to herself, at least.

'I promise,' Ivy said to Olivia now, 'no matter what happens in the future – whether your talent makes you a huge Hollywood star, or my V-ness takes me away again – one thing will never, ever change. I will *never* not be there for you, wherever we are in the world.'

'Oh, Ivy!' Olivia wrapped her up in a rib-crushing hug.

'Hey!' Ivy whispered, even as she sniffled back a tear. 'Maybe you *have* inherited some vampire strength, after all!'

'Um.' Holly coughed, just a foot or two away, and the two of them broke apart. 'I just wanted to say . . .' She looked out the window and winced. 'I'm so sorry for all the fuss I've caused in your home town. I never thought so many people would really believe in vampires, of all things!'

Ivy had to hide her grin behind an 'understanding' face. Poor Holly didn't realise just how much fuss she'd really caused – she had no idea that, right at this moment, she actually *was* surrounded by vampires. Holly would be shocked to know she'd been telling the truth on her blog all along!

Next to Ivy, though, Olivia looked grave. 'I'm not sure I liked all of your tactics,' she said. 'I mean, circulating anonymous Internet rumours is never a good idea . . . But I can kind of understand where you were coming from. Everybody wants their family to be happy.'

She shot Ivy a significant glance. Ivy stifled a sigh as she stepped towards Holly.

'Friends?' she said to her, stepping forwards.

Before Holly could answer, Olivia's cell phone rang. The sound made both twins freeze.

Ivy knew that pop-song ringtone. Olivia flushed, her eyes widening as she stared down at the ringing phone. Holly just looked confused. 'Um, aren't you going to answer that?' she asked.

'I . . .' Olivia took a deep breath. She straightened her shoulders. 'Yes, I am. I really am.' She pressed the button. 'Jackson,' she said. 'How are you?' The tone of her voice was as cool and confident as if she were talking to a stranger, but Ivy recognised the dreamy look in her eyes.

Ivy smirked and raised an eyebrow. 'Give him my love,' she whispered.

Olivia rolled her eyes at her twin, but her cheeks turned even deeper pink. She slid away through the crowd, clearly looking for a quiet spot.

'Who was that?' Holly asked.

'Olivia's ex-boyfriend,' Ivy said. But she couldn't help adding, 'At least, for now.'

Jackson had a funny habit of calling at all the right moments, didn't he? And now that the film industry strikes were over, *Eternal Sunset* could finally start shooting, with Olivia and Jackson starring in the lead roles . . . which meant that he and Olivia would be reunited soon, at least on a film set.

Jackson Caulfield hadn't become a Hollywood megastar for nothing. Ivy had a feeling he would know exactly how to romance Olivia on set, and she couldn't wait to see her sister brimming with real happiness again.

'Hey.' Brendan stepped up behind Ivy, draping an arm around her shoulders as Holly made a discreet exit. 'What's put that grin on your face?'

'Just thinking about the future.' She glanced at him, and gasped. 'Brendan! You're eating!'

'So?' He shrugged, and took another bite of the half-eaten burger in his hand. 'These are pretty good.'

'They ought to be,' Ivy said. 'I made them for you. See? I'm a fabulous cook too, just like you.' Smiling, she leaned into him, feeling the last of her tension melt away. Her boyfriend had got his appetite back at last, her grandmother was smiling at her from across the room, and Olivia was well on her way to happiness and the film career she'd always dreamed of.

'Happy?' Brendan asked.

'Pretty good,' Ivy admitted.

'Just "pretty good"?' Brendan laughed, as

he dropped a kiss on her hair. 'Come on, Vega. You may be the toughest of us all, but even you have to admit things couldn't get much better than this. Franklin Grove's secrets are safe, your grandmother seems to have forgiven you, your dad's about to get married again, *and* you and Olivia are back on track.'

'You're right,' Ivy said. 'That's not just good. It's *excellent*. And most important of all . . .' She turned around to face him, grinning.

'Yeah?' Brendan grinned back at her and polished off the last of his burger. 'What could be even better than all that?'

'After today,' Ivy said, 'I never have to see you wearing a button-down shirt again!'

Their laughter mingled as they kissed and, for once, Ivy didn't even care that everyone at the engagement party could see them together. As they turned, holding hands, to walk back into the thick of the party Ivy couldn't wait to see what the future held for all of them.

She squeezed Brendan's fingers, smiling.

Fingers crossed, no garlic!

TWIN TALK!

In the latest instalment of Georgia Huntingdon's interview series with Ivy and Olivia, she gets the scoop on the trickiest period of their turbulent year, which saw them having unwanted encounters with VITs!

Georgia Huntingdon: So your very eventful summer was nearly over, but – before it ended – I gather there were yet more adventures to be had.

Ivy Vega: I don't know if you'd call them 'adventures'.

Olivia Abbott: '*Mis*adventures', definitely.

Ivy: Except, I don't *miss* them.

Olivia: Groan! You've got a-PUN-dicitis again, sis!

Ivy: It's Brendan's fault. That boy is infectious.

Georgia: [laughs] We knew that!

Ivy: That's not what I meant.

Olivia: Do you notice how Ivy spends most of her time in these interviews blushing?

Ivy: One death-squint, coming right up.

Georgia: All right, all right. So, your summer?

Ivy: I'm sure you got the memo. Franklin Grove was completely crawling with VITs.

Georgia: I got one or two . . . *hundred* batsqueaks on the subject.

Olivia: I feel so terrible for not realising that Holly was up to something.

Ivy: It's nothing to feel bad about. I don't think Holly meant for things to get as out of control as they did. But that's what the VITs are like – they get amped up and go a little . . . crazy.

Georgia: Is it true what I was reading on the Vorld Vide Veb? That they were turning up at the mall wearing garlic necklaces?

Ivy: Please, don't . . . I've done enough dry-heaving for one lifetime. A *vampire* lifetime, too, which is much longer.

Georgia: Sounds like my worst nightmare.

Ivy: I swear, I can still feel the stench on me.

Olivia: I don't know why some bunnies get all excited about there being real vampires in the world. The VITs had this weird look – excited and scared all at the same time.

Georgia: I've seen that look on lots of people, all over the world.

Olivia: Is it wrong that I find VITs scarier than I find vamps?

Georgia: And this 'Holly' girl, how did all of that end?

Olivia: We're all friends now. Her dad's book has started to take off and he's getting a film deal, too.

Ivy: Holly was a little pesky, but she didn't *know* she was doing vampires any harm.

Olivia: Imagine if she knew how close she was to the truth!

Ivy: I'd rather not. If Holly *had* accidentally exposed the existence of vamps, I think those garlic necklaces would have gone on sale in stores! See, even *you* shuddered. Imagine the smell!

Olivia: I wasn't shuddering at *that* – I was disgusted at the thought of anyone wearing garlic as an accessory. What *would* it go with?

Ivy: [laughs] Your priorities will always be a mystery to me.

Georgia: You mentioned a film deal for Holly's dad. Staying with movies for the moment, I hear that the Hollywood strikes are over, which means . . .

Olivia: I know, I know!

Georgia: Is *Eternal Sunset* back on track?

Olivia: I think it's . . . Oh, gosh, I don't know if I'm allowed to say.

Ivy: Oh my darkness, how many times? VAMP magazine –

Olivia:— *knows how to keep a secret*. OK, OK. Since it's you guys, I guess there's no harm in telling. We're about to start filming soon.

Ivy: Tell her the best part.

Olivia: We get to shoot it in some great cities, all over the world! New York, Prague, *London* —

Ivy: No, not that. The *real* best part.

Olivia: I don't know what you mean.

Ivy: Oh, sis — if you're going to become a Hollywood megastar, you will *have* to give more convincing performances than *that*.

Georgia: What's the best part?

Ivy: We've seen the shooting schedule — Olivia and Jackson get to spend almost every day together for the entire production!

Georgia: *Now* who's blushing?

Olivia: Stop it, both of you.

Georgia: I just knew this story wasn't over!

Ivy: Although, Olivia, you must make sure he knows . . .

Olivia: Knows what?

Ivy: That, if he makes you cry again, he will have *me* to deal with.

Olivia: I can take care of myself.

Ivy: I know you can – but that doesn't mean I won't just take care of you anyway.

Olivia: It's all going to be fine. I think we'll be too busy working to create any off-camera drama.

Georgia: I can see that Ivy doesn't quite believe you.

Ivy: I think those two will always create drama. They are actors, after all!

Olivia: I guess we'll just have to wait and see, won't we?

Ivy: I guess we will.

Check back soon for more candid convos
with the world's most unlikely twins –
ONLY in VAMP magazine.